S<!---->in the Dark
and Other Twisted Tales

JEFF VANOUDENHOVE

JAVO PUBLICATION

Westfield, MA

Copyright © 2022 by Jeff VanOudenhove

No part of this book may be reproduced, distributed, or transmitted in any form without the express written consent of the publisher, except by a reviewer who wishes to quote brief passages in connection with a review written for inclusion in a magazine, newspaper, or website.

JAVO Publication
Westfield, Massachusetts 01085

This is a work of fiction. The characters, places, and events portrayed in this book are either the product of the author's imagination or are used fictitiously. Any similarity to real persons, living or dead, business establishments, or events is coincidental and not intended by the author.

ISBN 979-8-9865975-0-8

Library of Congress Control Number: 2022912969

Cover art by: Joseph Weymouth

The scanning, uploading, and distribution of this book via the internet or any other means without the permission of the publisher is illegal and punishable by law. Please purchase only authorized electronic editions, and do not participate or encourage electronic piracy of copyrighted materials. Your support of the author's rights is appreciated.

For Paul, Jeff, Kevin, Danielle, Nicolaas, and Emma, who I hope will one day read this and let me know I did a decent job with it.

Acknowledgments

I'd like to thank the Whipcity Wordsmiths for allowing me to try out a couple of these stories on them during our meetings. The feedback and encouragement I received from them are what help me keep doing what I'm doing.

I'd like to thank my Editor, Elizabeth Kelly, for the tremendous help she gave in making these stories better than they were when she first received them.

Thank you, Irina Lezhnyak, for being a beta reader for some of these stories. Your feedback and critique helped me better gauge how readers would respond to them.

These acknowledgments wouldn't be complete if I didn't give a heart-felt shout-out to Joe Weymouth, the incredible cover artist for this book. He should win a prize for the amazing work he has done on it.

And of course, I'd like to thank my wife, Elena, who has yet to tell me I need to stop with this book-writing nonsense (even if there were times she felt that way).

Introduction

What you hold in your hands is a book of truly twisted tales that will hold you in suspense until every last page. The stories within, designed purely for the intent of scaring, surprising, and enthralling you, are not for the faint of heart. Your breathing will become shallow as your chest tightens and squeezes the air from your lungs. Your heart will race with anticipation with each spine-tingling turn of the page. You will feel the sweat as it drips from your brow. Can you already feel the goosebumps forming on your arms, the hair tugging at your skin as it rises on the back of your neck? These are just a few of the side effects you should prepare yourself for as you delve deep into the weird tales of the mysterious and the macabre, of fearsome fright, bone-chilling horror, and strange deeds.

Draw the curtains, make yourself a cup of hot tea, curl up in your favorite chair under a warm blanket, and get ready to feel your senses reel. Without further ado, I present to you, Screams in the Dark.

Don't say you haven't been warned!

1

Behind Closed Doors

I'll never forget the day she disappeared. It was my eleventh birthday. It was supposed to be a great day. Now it's a day that will haunt me forever. How were we to know? We were so young, so believing. We were so naive. No, how could I ever forget the day she disappeared? After all, it was my fault.

For you to understand, I'd have to take you back; back to how it all began. It's not a pretty story. At least, I realize that now that I'm older. But back then, it was the only story I knew, and it was a happy one. It may sound confusing, but I'll do my best to explain.

It was late September of 1956 and unseasonably hot. It had been a scorcher all week, and the sweltering heat had found its way inside. Momma had the fan running constantly, but all it would do was circulate the already stale, humid air. Momma used to tell us we'd have to strip down to our underwear if we wanted to cool down. Some days we'd do it, Jenny and I. Jenny was my little sister. She was six years old. This story is about her.

She was a skinny, little thing but sharp as a tack. I figured she must have strayed from the shallow end of the gene pool where I was busy splashing away in all my glory. She had the brains; I had the bulk. I was five years older, so it was only natural that I was bigger than she was. But my age alone didn't account for my size. I was plump. I knew it; she knew it. I'm pretty sure Momma thought so too, though she'd never say it, not out loud, anyway. To her, I was always "precious" or "sweetie-pie." Poor Jenny was "little shit" or "damn kid."

At the time, I had no idea why I garnered the lion's share of Momma's love, and I didn't much care. Truthfully, I'm not sure I noticed as much back then. It was what I was used to, so it all seemed normal. It's funny what a child thinks "normal" is when it's all they've known.

It never bothered me when I'd come home from school and see Momma standing over Jenny, telling her that she needed to do a better job scrubbing the floors. I just thought it was how things were. Plus, it meant it was one less thing I had to do. Why would I cause a fuss over it?

It wasn't just the floors; it was the windows, the dishes, and even the toilet, too. Momma had Jenny doing all of it.

The dishes had to be spotless before they could be put into the cabinet. And they *were*, too. Jenny knew the price she'd pay if even a single blemish remained on a dish.

The toilet had to be cleaned every day. Momma used to say that there wasn't anything in life much better than being able to sit on a fresh bowl. Jenny used to make it shine for fear of getting her behind beaten if she hadn't. Momma could be strict that way.

When it came to the windows, with the cloudy residue clinging to them, Momma was more lenient since they were difficult to wash, what with the bars being in the way and all. She had the black, iron accents installed on all of them a few years earlier after some hooligans had broken into the house. I didn't remember that, but she said it was an awful experience; it's why she had special locks installed on all the doors too.

For all of Momma's seeming mistreatment of Jenny during those years, she was protective too. Unlike with me, she chose to homeschool Jenny. She used to say it was because she needed someone around to help her with the household chores, but I knew it was because she was nervous and afraid of others harming her delicate little girl, especially after what had happened with Karen. That was my older sister that I never had the opportunity to meet.

Anyway, it was during Jenny's homeschooling that she first learned about the terrible thing hiding in her bedroom closet. I remember when Momma first told *me* about it back when I occupied that room. It caused me many sleepless nights thinking about what it was that lurked behind that locked door. I had never seen it, but I knew it was real, or at least, it was my youthful ignorance that made me believe that. How could I not? After all, it was Karen's room before it was mine, and look what happened to her when Momma accidentally left the closet door unlocked one night. That thing…it took her, and she was never seen or heard from again. After I had learned about that tragic incident, I couldn't wait to get out of there.

I was relieved when Jenny came along. Momma relocated me to the larger room across the hall. Her new baby girl didn't need such a space, and since Karen's room still had all the effects of a little girl's room, even during my occupancy (I wasn't allowed to change anything), it seemed like a natural fit.

I should have been more concerned that the latest addition to our family was being placed in the same room where a killer beast resided behind a single closed door only ten feet from her, but at the time, I was only thinking about self-preservation.

So, what *was* it that was in the closet, you ask? I wish I could answer that, but as I mentioned, I had never seen it. Momma knows; she had seen it several times over the years, slinking about when it thought she wasn't around. She'd tell me stories of how the darkness itself would come alive and take physical shape, transformed into a wretched four-legged creature that preyed on innocent children during the night. It wasn't an animal, such as a rabid dog or wild bear, but something else, something *evil*. It was more humanoid in appearance but chose to walk on all fours rather than remain bipedal. The swirling darkness that made up its body dripped from its being like black ooze. Its eyes were red, and the noise from its jagged teeth constantly slamming into each other as its jaw opened and closed in rapid succession was like fingernails nervously tapping on a hardened surface. Even today, the thought of it makes my skin crawl.

The horrible, child-stealing monster only ever came out at night, but Momma chose to keep the closet door locked at all times. Even during the daylight hours, she was the only one allowed to go into the large, walk-in closet. She kept the key on her at all times to ensure nobody was allowed access into the wicked fiend's lair.

Now and again, I had the opportunity to peek inside when Momma would go to put the laundry away or to pull out the next day's school clothes for me, which is something she had always done when the room was mine. She had done the same for Jenny once the room was hers, always choosing the next day's wardrobe for her and laying them out on the dresser. Only Momma ever went into the closet; the thing wouldn't dare come out if it knew an adult was present.

During the day, while Momma fussed over the laundry, and I would get the chance to catch a glimpse into the disgusting creature's den, it never seemed that foreboding, especially when the morning sun's rays would shine through the lone window located within, splashing across Momma as she sorted the clothes. I remember thinking how the window seemed out of place, situated inside a closet between two large shelving units where layers of folded clothes resided. But Momma later explained to me how, what was now the closet, had once been part of the main bedroom. The previous owners had enclosed an area inside the room, turning it into a walk-in wardrobe. That helped explain why the bedroom always felt so small.

After Momma told Jenny about the creature, something changed in my little sister. When our bedroom doors were open, I had a clear view into Jenny's room. She didn't know it, but I would see her constantly staring at the closet door with something serious in her eyes, perhaps best described as a look of morbid curiosity. It wasn't fear, at least not the same look of fear as when Momma would raise her hand at her, threatening to tan her hide for disobeying an order, but I could tell the wheels were spinning in that little head of hers. Even at bedtime, I would sometimes see Jenny bundled under her blanket, the covers gripped tightly in her hands and pulled up to her chin as she lay there, her eyes focused on the closed door at the far wall. I can't imagine the thoughts that must have been swirling around in that poor girl's head. But then Momma would come to say her final good night and close our doors. I would hear her lock Jenny's, but mine remained unlocked. I guess it was because I was older.

On more than one occasion, I had woken to strange noises coming from Jenny's room. I'd quietly creep from my bedroom and press my ear against her locked door to hear what it was all about. I couldn't be positive, but it sounded like a doorknob jostling, like that thing in the closet was trying to get out. Jenny never made a noise. I didn't know if it was because she was too gripped with fear, her voice unable to sound out, or if she was more afraid of waking Momma in the middle of the night. Both were terrifying thoughts.

Each morning, when Momma unlocked her door, Jenny would come rushing out of the room like she was on fire, scrambling to make it to the bathroom before wetting herself. Poor kid must have been holding it all night, but she knew better than to cry out.

One time, while I was intently listening to the creature vigorously struggle with the knob and fearing it was going to break free, I called out to Jenny, hoping she'd respond or at least be comforted by the sound of my voice. She didn't answer, but the jiggling sound of the doorknob suddenly ceased, and I could hear the rustling sound of the bed coverings flopping about as if Jenny had suddenly become restless. I guess I can understand why; my carrying voice had disturbed Momma's sleep.

She came up the stairs, her eyes puffy and bloodshot, a look of bitter annoyance on her face. When she saw me standing in the hall beside Jenny's door, Momma's expression suddenly changed to that of utter disapproval. I'll never forget her words when I told her I had heard the creature trying to escape from its closet prison.

"Then, I can't blame my precious boy for something that's going on in Jenny's room, now can I? But someone's gotta pay for waking me up."

When Momma unlocked and opened the door to step inside, I saw the tears beginning to form in Jenny's eyes even as Momma slowly closed the door behind her, preventing me from seeing the beating that was about to take place. After the sound of the first slap, I ran to my room, shut the door, and covered my ears. Momma must have been tired that night for her to unload on Jenny as she did. But, after that incident, I learned to keep my mouth shut whenever I heard the evil presence rattling the doorknob. I got through those tough nights by convincing myself that as long as the creature stayed locked away in that closet, Jenny would remain safe. And she did; until I screwed everything up.

It all started about a week before my eleventh birthday. I was in an irritable mood when I came home from school because Tommy Streeter had stolen a Mickey Mantle baseball card from my bag. I knew he had done it, but I couldn't prove it. The teacher looked in Tommy's locker and lunchbox but didn't find it, so she had no reason to believe he had taken it. She let him go without so much as a warning. I got spoken to about it, though. Mrs. Peppan shook her finger at me and warned me about playing practical jokes for the sake of trying to get others in trouble. Even though I pleaded with her to listen to me, she still thought I was lying about the incident. Even today, the image of Tommy's face as he smugly snickered at me while walking away still lingers in my brain. But on *that* day, I couldn't bear it.

When I got home, I was fuming. As soon as I walked in the door, I threw my stuff down and ran up to my room. Jenny was already in there, sitting on my bed and playing with my can of Play-doh. It wasn't anything to get mad about; I often found her in my room playing since she didn't like being alone in hers, but when I saw her playing with my stuff, all I could think about was Tommy taking what was mine, and at that moment, in my mind, Jenny was taking from me too.

"Stop touching my things!" I yelled. "And play in your own room!"

I shouldn't have shouted at her like that, but something inside me snapped, and I had to let my pent-up frustration out on somebody. She was just the unlucky one I came across first. I knew I had startled her since she leaped from my bed as quickly as she could, wide-eyed and flush. She put her head down and quietly walked past me. Just as she made it to the door, I gave her a little shove in the back, pushing her toward her room. Understandably, she got upset with my uncalled-for, childish action and ran back to me, kicked me in my shin, and scampered to her room, shutting the door behind her. I don't remember her kick hurting me all that much, but I was furious and didn't want to let it go.

Usually, my temper never lasted more than a couple of hours, but the moment had gripped me, and it continued its hold on me long after the night had turned into day. I knew I was acting awful to Jenny each day after that, but I couldn't bring myself to stop.

Oh, I could sit here and blame it on the heat; Lord knows the temperature had many folks acting out, but that wouldn't be fair to her memory. It was all me, all the way. The thing is, my birthday was coming, and although I knew Momma was going to buy me a present of some kind, here I was, having just had my favorite baseball card stolen from me, and nobody cared a lick. It just wasn't fair.

I didn't treat Jenny very nice over that week leading up to my birthday. Maybe it was selfishness. Maybe, I was just a little prick. More than likely, it was a combination of the two. And as my birthday approached, I became harsher toward her. I saw her face change over those six long days. Where once in her eyes there had been tender innocence and youthful admiration toward me, now only displayed a look of mournful hopelessness. It was as if she thought the one person she could count on had left her. And it didn't even bother me.

Had I known what was going to happen, I'd take it all back. It's too late now, though, and Jenny paid the price. I don't know why I did it. As I said, I was a little prick, I guess. At the time, I think I only meant it to be a joke. I thought it would be funny if I put a little scare in Jenny.

It was the afternoon before my birthday, and Momma was in Jenny's room putting the laundry away. Jenny was in the kitchen, washing the last of the dishes. I had followed Momma upstairs, knowing exactly where she was going and what she'd be doing, but I stopped off in my room first. I had to get some Scotch tape. When I joined Momma in Jenny's room, she was so busy folding and putting the clothes neatly on the shelves in the closet that she didn't notice me peeking my head around the open door. I wasn't interested in looking for the dreadful creature that lurked within, I knew it wouldn't be there since it was still light out and the late afternoon sun was shining its rays through the closet window. Instead, my focus was on Momma. I didn't want her to see what I was about to do.

The idea had come to me during lunch. I had mentioned how I still hadn't gotten my baseball card back, and Jenny made a comment that riled me. She said, "It's just a baseball card; you have plenty of others."

It's true; it was just a baseball card. But it was a Mickey Mantle baseball card, and to a boy at eleven years old, it was everything.

"Shut up, pipsqueak," I returned. "At least I'm not afraid of every little noise in my room."

"I'm not scared!" she shouted back.

"You are so," I said. "You think that thing in your closet is gonna eat you in the night."

"I am not!" she raised her voice a second time. "I'm not scared of the closet monster."

"The two of you better shut your traps," Momma jumped in, "before I slap the words out of your mouths. And you, you little piss ant," she continued while pointing her butterknife at Jenny, "you *should* be afraid of what's in your closet. It'll come out and get you like it did your sister."

After that comment, the two of us remained quiet for the rest of the meal, but an idea had already been planted in my brain; I'd show *her*.

 For the plump kid that I was, I could be pretty stealthy when the situation called for it. Momma didn't notice me peering into the closet while she was busy with the clothes, and she certainly didn't notice me place a piece of tape over the latch plate in the door frame. She would've had my hide if she did.

I slithered back to my room, where I eventually heard the familiar sound of Momma locking the closet door when she was through. Only, it *hadn't* locked because of my carefully-placed piece of tape.

Once dusk came upon us, and it was time for bed, Jenny took to her room, and I lay in bed listening for any unusual sounds that might escape from under her door. What I was eagerly waiting for was to hear her scream at the first creak of the closet door opening, anticipating her banging on her bedroom door and wanting to take shelter in mine. I knew Momma would come and rescue her, but I wanted to rub it in Jenny's face. The moment wasn't coming fast enough. I thought I heard her scampering around her room at one point, but then all went silent again. I didn't think much of it; I just kept waiting for the loud shriek that never seemed to come. Without realizing it, I dozed off.

I *did* eventually wake to the sound of the hysterical screaming that I had craved, but it wasn't from Jenny; it was Momma, instead. I quickly jumped out of bed, my heart threatening to burst through my chest. When I opened my door and bounded across the hallway into the doorway of Jenny's room, I saw Momma on her knees, crumpled to the floor near the gaping maw of the foreboding closet.

It was daytime, the sun's soothing rays exploding through the closet window, vanquishing any evil within; the threat had passed. The creature had come and gone in the nighttime hours, and Jenny, my dear sister, was nowhere to be found. She had been taken by the vile shadow beast that came alive in the night, swallowed whole by its insatiable hunger.

I didn't mean for it to happen that way. I only wanted to scare Jenny a bit. She was supposed to scream if the creature came for her. Momma would have protected her from it. But it was a stealthy hunter with centuries of practice. It knew how to steal children in the silent hours. Jenny had only been its latest victim. Happy frickin' birthday to me.

Don't worry, though; it didn't all end as badly as you might think. Sure, it was a rough couple of months after that horrible incident, but things eventually returned to normal, especially after I got another sister. Momma even let me help pick her out that time.

Sweet Margie lasted longer than Jenny did before the night creature got her in the end, too. Then, there was Susie, but she was only my sister for a couple of weeks before the bad men with the shiny badges came and took Momma from us. That was a low point in my life. I *did* manage to move on, however.

I'm old in years now, but way back then, Momma had taught me what I needed to know. It's why I'm telling you this now. It's why I'm showing you the inside of the closet. There's nothing for you to be afraid of anymore; I've gotten rid of the danger. You see, when Momma had the bars installed on all the windows those many years ago, she had forgotten about the window in the closet. Out of sight, out of mind, I guess. I reckon that's how the creature kept getting in and taking my sisters. Momma thought locking the closet door would keep us safe. It didn't.

As you can see, I've since had bars added, and the window has been permanently sealed. There's nothing for you to worry about; you're safe. Now you can rest easy, knowing there's nothing evil behind this closed door. And after today, you'll have a little sister to play with too. I'm gonna find a nice one for you tomorrow morning. Won't that be fun? Then you'll both be safe for a long, long time.

2

Crawl Space

The smell of methane gas mixed with a hint of sulfur permeated the tiny passageway. It stung Drake's nose. There was barely enough room to move, but he somehow managed to negotiate the entire length of the suffocating cavern by crawling on his stomach. He traversed it many times, in fact. There was no way out.

How long had it been since he had found himself trapped within the rocky confines of the darkened cave, having had to contort his body to squeeze into the unforgiving tunnel? Though there seemed to be no visible light source, the glow from the phosphorescent rocks continued to shimmer through the passage, letting him at least see his next meal. It was a beetle. It wouldn't have been his first choice, but the menu was limited. The rats only lasted so long. Before that, the only thing that sustained him was the colony of bats that found themselves unfortunate enough to be trapped within the same claustrophobic space. He wished it hadn't come to that; he thought he'd find a way out. When he realized there was none, and the hunger eventually became unbearable, it was them or him. The choice was simple once laid out rationally.

He had come across their nest the first time he shimmied his way to the far end of the constricting corridor of rock. There were hundreds of them, perhaps even thousands, huddled together in massive blankets of wings and fur. At first, he stared in admiration as they slept, nestled together like newborn puppies clumped against their mother's comforting warmth. Where did they come from, he wondered? He had traveled the complete distance of the tunnel and had seen no visible way out. Then, as if responding to his unspoken question, he watched as a slew of them crawled in through a small crack in the cave's ceiling to join with their brothers.

When night would fall upon the outside world, the bats would evacuate the passage, en masse, to hunt for their meals, leaving the tiny cavern silent and still. Drake had taken that time to try and dig at the crack in the ceiling, but it was no use. The rock formation wouldn't give, save for a small shard that had broken free in his first attempt at clawing at the hard surface.

He would later use that splinter of stone to kill his first meal.

He held out as long as he could, but starvation was not the way he had ever pictured his life coming to an end. When the hunger took control of his senses, he waited for the first bat to return to its lair.

It was a small one, but it would do. As it squeezed its tiny body through the crevice, Drake smashed it with the piece of rock he had saved. If he had waited for the bat to fully emerge from the tiny gap in the rock chamber, he risked it flying off or possibly scratching at him. Best to take it swiftly and without the risk.

It wasn't the worst meal he had ever had, and looking at the beetle he now held in his palm, he longed for the taste of the bat. They had sustained him for quite some time. He had learned to ration his meals, taking only two bats a day when his appetite was at its most ferocious. In time, when he noticed the colony was thinning, he had no choice but to reduce his intake to only one per day. With nobody coming to rescue him from the compressive tomb he was trapped in, the bats were only ever going to last so long.

Then, there were the rats. The first one showed up about a week after the last bat had been consumed. It was like they knew the bats were gone, and they were coming to take shelter in the vacated nest. It was the lingering smell of the bones that had attracted them. They scampered in from an opening at the base of the cave wall, infiltrating the small space in a hostile takeover. They came in droves to pick at the bat bones, feasting on scraps and morsels left behind. Drake was happy they had.

Weak and emaciated, he stabbed into one of the rodents with the sharp rock he maintained, taking no time to feed on its freshly dead carcass. The meat wasn't as tasty as the bats, but there was more of it. The rats were quite plump. It was clear they hadn't missed any meals.

After eating his first rat, Drake quickly ripped a portion of his shirt off and plugged the hole where the rats had entered. After all, he didn't want his dinner escaping.

He killed a few of them immediately, devouring them in minutes as if he'd never had a meal before. Then, the portioning began. Like he had done with the bats, Drake would kill and eat only one rat a day to fulfill his need for sustenance (though with the bats gone, it was difficult for Drake to tell when it was the next day). There weren't as many rats, and they needed to last as long as possible. He had no idea how long he was going to remain confined within the dank walls of the small chamber. The cave could, quite possibly, become his literal tomb.

Between meals, Drake had continued to slither and squeeze his way back and forth through the tunnel, hoping to come across a means of escape, perhaps something he'd missed on his many such travels. Each journey led to the same dead-end, another hopeless effort. How much longer would he have to wait before someone liberated him, he wondered? At least he had his meals to look forward to until his hopeful rescue.

With his food supply diminishing, Drake soon opted to eat only once every *other* day. It had only made sense; the rats were fat enough, at least twice the meat as the bats had to offer. But eventually, they too were gone.

He removed the piece of fabric he had used to block the rat entrance in hopes that the enticing aroma of the fresh pile of bones would attract some more four-legged food into his prison. It wasn't a bad idea, and there were a few furry stragglers that had wandered in, in search of nourishment, but nothing that lasted for what Drake needed to survive.

Another week had passed, and desperation gripped him tightly in its grasp. His stomach ached, wrenching and twisting, tying his insides in knots. He needed something (anything) to get him through another day. He needed food. It's what prompted him to even consider feasting on the insect that, at that very moment, was scrambling around in his lightly clenched fist.

Opening his hand and plucking the brown-colored beetle between his index finger and thumb, Drake stared at it as it wriggled in his fingers, its legs running a marathon in place. He shook his head in disgust and opened his mouth, letting his tongue extend to accept the struggling bug. But before he plopped the diminutive pest into his waiting maw, a clanking sound acquired his attention, causing him to drop the insect. He stayed motionless, watching his not-so-delectable treat scurry away into a crack in the floor while he held his breath, listening for the returning sound.

Clank!

There it was again, he thought. It was coming from behind him.

Clank, clank!

And again. Another couple of sharp bangs. It sounded like metal cracking against the surface of the rock. Drake excitedly wobbled his body backward through the tunnel, slowly sliding himself to where the entrance had been sealed off.

Clank, clank!

Clank, clank!

More banging. The sound was louder now; he was getting close. He couldn't believe it; someone had found him.

Clank, clank, clank!

"Hello," a voice rang out. "Is somebody in there?"

"Yes!" Drake called out, stomping his foot against the rock wall behind him. "Yes, I'm in here. I've been trapped with no way out. Help me!"

"Ok," yelled the voice, "I'm gonna get you out of there. Just hang tight, ok?"

"I've got nothing better to do," Drake replied with a slight giggle in his voice, unbelieving that he was finally being released.

Clank, clank!

The sound reverberated through the tunnel as the rescuer's pickaxe slammed into the solid wall of rock, sending pieces of debris crashing to the cavern floor. Drake felt himself beginning to quiver in anticipation of the sealed entrance crumbling under the constant battery from the hardened steel of the pickaxe.

Clank, clank! Clank, clank!

Again and again, a barrage of blows against the cavern's exterior wall continued until, at last, a hole was punctured in the rocky face, sending a rush of air and dust into the small tunnel. Drake took in a deep breath, drawing the oxygen deep into his lungs until they began to burn. He didn't care; it still felt better than breathing the stale, methane-filled air he had been forced to suffer through for far too long.

The man on the outside peeked in through the hole he had created, "You all right in there, mister? Are you injured at all?"

"No, no," Drake replied. "I'm not injured. I was when I first found myself trapped in here, but it's been a long time. I'm ok now. Thank goodness you arrived when you did."

"Well, hang on," the stranger stated, "you're almost home free. A few more solid hits should do it. If you can move forward a bit... I wouldn't want any of these rocks falling on you when I bust through."

"Will do," Drake responded as he slithered forward a few feet.

Clank, clank, clank!

In a few minutes, and with a thunderous roar, the rock wall gave way, showering the cavern and passageway in a plume of dust. As it began to settle, Drake wriggled his way, feet-first, toward the opening until his savior was able to grab ahold of his legs and pull him free from his long stay in the narrow catacomb.

Unable to keep his footing, drake fell to the floor and sat upright, wiping his thin face with his shirt sleeve.

"You don't look so good, mister," the man said. "How long have you been trapped in there?"

"Honestly," Drake replied, breathing heavily, "I have no idea. It feels like it's been years. How did you know I was in there, anyway?"

"I didn't," the man said. "I came into this series of caverns to do some exploring. I noticed a piece of fabric sticking out of the wall, wedged between some of the rocks, so I started digging, not knowing what I would find."

Drake looked down at his pant leg, a large section of material torn from it.

"Well, will you look at that?" he stated while shaking his head in disbelief. "I never even knew my pants had ripped. I guess I'm lucky they did."

"I guess so," the man replied, extending his hand to help Drake to his feet. "You're looking pretty thin. You must be famished."

Drake clasped the man's hand and pulled himself up, using the man's weight to stabilize himself under his feet.

"Believe it or not," Drake answered, "I feel like I've had enough to eat. I'm more thirsty than anything else."

With that, Drake opened his mouth, exposing the fangs sprouting from his gums, and chomped onto the man's neck. Ripping the flesh aside as the man howled in excruciating pain, Drake buried his fangs ever deeper, drinking from the throbbing jugular until the stranger was depleted of all life.

As the man's lifeless body fell to the floor, Drake licked his lips clean of the scarlet liquid he needed to sustain his life. The rats and the bats played their part, keeping him alive while he was trapped, but now he was free again. The human imbeciles had buried him, thinking to end his ceaseless thirst for blood. They were fools. They should have plunged a stake through his heart and ended him forever. Nevermore would he need to drink from the likes of the vermin he was confined with. Those creatures were not worthy enough to have one such as he feed upon them. He now had bigger meals on which to prey. The son of Dracula was no longer contained, and the human race would pay dearly with their blood.

3

Freaky Friday

Peter stared into the officer's eyes as if he didn't quite comprehend what he had been asked. He saw the lips moving; he could hear jumbled sounds, but it sounded as though he had cotton stuffed in his ears. He reached up with his cuffed, bloody hands and wiped away the sweat that had gathered on his forehead, leaving behind streaks of the crimson fluid instead. The officer repeated himself.

"Can you tell us again what happened? Why don't you start at the beginning?"

Peter looked down at his blood-stained shirt, the vibrant red blotches painting a vivid picture on a blank canvas, and he wondered how difficult it would be to get the stain out in the wash. He lifted his head back to the officer sitting across from him, realizing he was still waiting for an answer. A second officer was behind the first, leaning against the pale gray walls of the tiny room, his arms folded about his chest. The question asked of him was an easy one, to which there was an even easier answer. But would they believe him?

Peter looked to his left at the closed door. He knew his only chance of being released was to lay it all out for the officers so they would understand. He reflected on the events leading up to this moment and pondered where to begin. The officer had asked for him to start at the beginning, but he couldn't be sure exactly when the beginning was. He knew it had been at least five days prior as he let his thoughts and words wander back on the recent past.

Monday
Everyone seemed to be in a chipper mood when Peter arrived at the office. It was in contrast to the previous week when everyone had been putting in overtime trying to meet their deadlines, their grumpy demeanors and unwarranted, rude comments toward their coworkers revealing, perhaps, fragments of their true selves. At least, that's what Peter thought before that Monday.

He had always been the last to arrive, choosing to sleep in as long as possible while the world around him woke to the first rays of the sun. There was a strange atmosphere about the place as soon as he walked in. The usual sound of fingers tapping away on keyboards, phones ringing off the hook, and at least one employee getting reprimanded by the office supervisor weren't heard as he made his way through the maze of cubicle walls. Instead, there was a quiet calmness that made him feel strangely uncomfortable. It was as though the usual hustle and bustle of the department suddenly ceased the moment he walked through the doors. As if that weren't peculiar enough, the staff seemed to stand as one, peering at him over their respective walls to greet him with blank stares and uncharacteristic, forced smiles. They said nothing, only awkwardly gazing as he quickly scurried past them to his familiar cube, burying his chin to his chest to keep from making eye contact.

As soon as he sat at his desk, he heard the sudden commotion of everyone else around him plopping themselves into their chairs and beginning to type away feverishly, finally showing signs of normalcy at that early hour. It was a bit odd, for sure, what had taken place, but the rest of the day seemed to continue without any further idiosyncrasies, so Peter wiped it clear from his mind. That is, until…

Tuesday
The numbers on his screen weren't adding up, and he wondered if he would be the next associate called into the supervisor's office for mishandling the accounts. Harsh verbal punishments were routine at Hammond and Fincher; doled out like candy, only much less sweet.

Peter leaned back in his chair, taking a quick break to collect his thoughts, and rubbed his eyes to clear away the blur in his vision he'd been noticing of late from constantly focusing on his monitor screen. So distracted by his latest concerns, he hadn't heard Roger step into his space behind him until the man's words, "Hey, Peter," startled him, causing his upper body to jerk forward in his chair. Peter swiveled around to see his neighboring coworker weirdly smirking, similar to what he had witnessed from the entire staff the day before.

"What is it, Roger?" Peter asked.

He received no response, just more of the same gawky smile that plagued Rogers' unshaven face, which, in itself, was an unusual sight since Peter had never once seen Roger with so much as a stray stubble occupying his chin.

"Come on, Roger, what do you want?" Peter urged with slight agitation in his voice. "I've got work to do."

Roger widened his eyes and began nodding like a dashboard bobblehead.

"Friday, huh, buddy?" Roger responded before turning and exiting Peter's cubicle.

Confused by the comment, Peter's eyes narrowed, trying to understand what it meant. He turned back to his computer and checked his email, first clicking on his personal calendar to see if he had perhaps forgotten about a meeting set up for that day. His schedule was clear. But then, when he checked the group calendar, he noticed someone had anonymously attached a link.

That must be what Roger's mysterious message was about, he thought and clicked on the link, which brought up a picture of a skull and crossbones with the words "Die, Die, Die" below it.

"Ha, ha. Very funny, guys," Peter mumbled to himself. He stood up to question Roger over his wall but saw that Roger wasn't at his desk. He scanned over the cubes to his left toward the conference room, where, situated in front of the large windows, the watercooler and coffee station resided. Roger was standing with Evelyn, at first unaware Peter had spied them from a distance until Roger pointed as if to direct her to his location. When the two had gleaned Peter staring at them, their eyes widened, and the awkward smile returned to their faces as their heads began to bobble incessantly, just as Roger's had done moments before. Peter quickly ducked behind his cubicle wall and sat back in his chair, his thoughts running wild while his fingers tapped nervously on his desk.

"Why the hell are people acting so weird around here?" Peter questioned under his breath.

Just then, Stan, the division supervisor, slapped his palm on the side of Peter's cubicle entrance, garnering his attention.

"Peter, I'll need those reports on my desk before Die-day."

Peter felt a chill run down his spine. "Wh-what did you just say, Stan?"

"I said, 'I'll need those reports on my desk before Friday.' You can get them done, can't you?"

"Y-yes, sir," Peter replied, nodding his head. "I'll have them to you before then."

"Good," Stan responded, "because Friday's a big day." Then he walked away, leaving Peter to contemplate, once again, what was happening on Friday.

The end of the day was drawing near, and he couldn't waste any more time pondering what the end of the week would bring. He needed to get his reports straightened out before submitting them to Stan. It wouldn't look good if his figures were off. He'd crunch the numbers again to see if he could locate the error, but his concentration was lacking. He needed to put all thoughts about Friday out of his mind. Whatever was going on that day couldn't concern him at the moment. He'd make sure to ask one of his coworkers about it in the morning.

Wednesday
Peter was running a little late and headed straight for his little slice of paradise within the offices of Hammond and Fincher, paying little attention to his peers on his way through the rows of beige-colored, textile walls. He shouldn't have stayed up as late as he had, but he couldn't get his mind off the strange behavior of his coworkers or their references to something taking place on the coming Friday. It bothered him that he couldn't recall what it was; he was usually pretty good about keeping track of things like that. It would have been understandable had he been able to blame it on having been absent the day it was discussed, only he

hadn't missed a day of work in over five months, not since his wife left him. If anything, he was *overworked*, but he didn't mind; it was his way of coping with suddenly being on his own again.

He had stayed at work late the night before, trying to correct the errors he had noticed on his accounts but was unsuccessful. That, too, weighed heavily on his mind, which contributed to at least a few hours of the previous night's bout of insomnia.

While Peter waited for his computer to boot up, he could hear muted whispers coming from all around him but decided to ignore them to focus on at least one unresolved item of business that plagued his sleepless night: finding out about Friday. He stood and glanced over his wall into Roger's cubicle to find that his neighbor wasn't present. That wasn't anything unusual; Roger could often be found down on the first floor, chatting it up with one of the women in the Finance Department. He was quite a flirt.

Peter decided to walk over to Norm's cube just beyond Roger's to retrieve the answers he sought. If anyone could enlighten him, it was Norm. The man had a nasty habit of sticking his nose in everyone's business, and he had no qualms about throwing his two cents into the mix if he felt his opinion was the only one that mattered…which, of course, was *always*. He had the scoop on everything that went on in the office, sometimes learning about policy changes before even the supervisor had received notice from Corporate.

Peter knocked on the top plastic trim of Norm's cubicle wall to get the balding man's attention. The last thing he wanted was to scare the man who had already had emergency bypass surgery a year earlier due to having a heart attack. At the sound of the knock, Norm swung his chair around to welcome his guest.

"Oh, hey, Peter," Norm greeted pleasantly, "what can I do for you?"

An outsider wouldn't know by hearing it, but it was a very unusual greeting from Norm, who preferred to call everyone "buddy" or "pal" or "chief" or some other such nickname. Peter had thought the man never cared enough to learn anyone's name and certainly hadn't ever called Peter by *his* first name.

"Norm, hey, sorry to bother you," Peter said reservedly. "I was just wondering about this Friday…"

He didn't get a chance to continue as Norm perked right up in his seat, interrupting Peter in mid-sentence.

"Yeah, yeah," he said enthusiastically. "I'm all set with my part. The plan is coming together. The takeover is *going* to happen."

"Takeover?" Peter questioned. "What are you talking about?"

Suddenly, Norm's expression soured as his eyebrows dipped in anger. He spun his chair around to his desk, and then, a moment later, spun back around to face Peter, only this time with the similar awkward smile on his face that Peter had witnessed from his other coworkers.

"Hey there, Sport," Norm greeted a second time in his more usual manner, "What can I help you with?"

"What do you mean?" Peter asked, slightly perturbed. "We were just talking about Friday?"

"No, I'm sorry, Buddy; you must be mistaken." Norm began bobbing his head back and forth before turning back to his computer.

"But you... I..."

"You're mistaken, champ," Norm reiterated, raising his hand above his shoulder to dismiss his guest.

Left speechless by the sudden change in Norm's behavior, Peter walked away, scratching his head, unable to quell the non-existent itch. On his way back to his office space, he paused and glanced over at the conference room, where he noticed a handful of coworkers had gathered just inside the open doorway. Staff meetings usually took place on Thursdays, not Wednesdays, so he wondered if he had missed an early-morning email invite by having his impromptu visit with Norm. He decided he would meander over to see what it was about, but when he got beyond the last row of cubicles, all eyes in the room turned with blank stares in his direction, save for the supervisor, who glared at him anxiously before closing the door.

Peter stopped, stunned at the reaction. He tilted his head sideways to peek around the solid door and through the window to see several of the employees pointing at him and smiling forcedly, making him feel very uncomfortable. He quickly turned his eyes away and instantly made an about-face, accidentally slamming into Roger, who was, at that moment, walking by.

"Whoa there, Peter," Roger chimed in, seeing how excited his coworker appeared. "Slow down before you hurt yourself."

"Sorry, Roger. I didn't see you there. Hey, tell me, what's going on in there?" He nodded sideways toward the conference room.

"Oh, that?" Roger responded. "They're getting ready for the communication."

"What communication?" Peter asked.

"You know, the signal." Roger pointed upward. "From up there."

Peter shifted his eyes to the ceiling, letting them wander from side to side, confused about what he was supposed to be seeing.

"I don't understand; what signal are you talking about?" He lowered his eyes back to Roger, who stood silently, bobbing his head back and forth, suddenly afflicted with the same ungainly smile as the others.

"Don't you think you should be getting back to your desk now, Peter?" Roger urged. "You'll want to make sure your numbers are correct before Friday."

Peter couldn't muster any words for the first few seconds, his mouth agape, until finally, inelegantly, he managed to squeak out a few.

"Uh, yeah. Right. I-I'll do that."

He slowly walked back to his desk, looking behind him only once to see nothing had changed in Roger's unusual expression.

For the rest of the workday, Peter kept to himself at his desk, struggling to concentrate, the continued whispers of his coworkers inexorably finding ways over and around his cubicle walls. He knew something strange was going on, something he had no control over. And that was something he didn't like at all.

Thursday

It had to be what he was thinking; there was no other reasonable explanation (as if what he was thinking was even remotely "reasonable"). He had stayed up most of the night, dwelling on the comments made by Norm and Roger that had him thoroughly perplexed. He believed he had it all figured out.

When he stepped out of the elevator that morning, a renewed confidence in his stride, he kept his chin up and his senses on high alert. Scanning the office through suspicious lenses, Peter was bound to pick up on the subtle differences he'd noticed in his coworkers' unusual behaviors. Whether he wanted to believe it or not, something didn't feel right.

Glimpsing Stan sitting at his desk through the partially opened doorway, he marched right into the supervisor's office and shut the door behind him.

"Stan, what's been going on around here?" Peter questioned sternly, pointing at other staff members through the office's floor-to-ceiling windows. "And don't even tell me you don't know what I'm talking about, the way everyone's been acting around here; it's very strange. Even the way Gloria's been acting, and you know how quiet she is, with how she's been traipsing about the office, stomping her feet as she walks by and continuously nodding her head and smiling mischievously. It's kinda freaky."

"Sshhh. Quiet!" Stan said excitedly while tamping his palms in the air to calm Peter. "Keep it down! If the others overhear, there's no telling what they might do."

"So, there *is* something going on, then? I knew it."

"But you mustn't let on that you know," Stan added. "If they find out you're not one of them, or if they think you'll stand in their way..."

"What?" Peter questioned. "Who are they? What's going on?"

"I think you've already figured it out," Stan answered. "Just as I had done a few days ago."

"You mean, they're...?" Peter went silent for a moment, glancing out the office window at his peers as they sauntered to and fro, pretending to carry out their mundane daily routines.

"That's right, Peter; they're from..." Stan stopped speaking, instead, letting his index finger complete the sentence as he pointed upward toward the ceiling, his eyes rolling up to follow. Peter understood Stan was referencing a location far beyond the limitations of the immediate structure overhead. He meant they had come from the far reaches of space.

Aliens!

"I knew it," Peter stated with nervous excitement. "I fucking knew it! They were all acting batty as hell. Shit, shit! What do they want? What do we do?"

"Calm down, Peter," Stan replied, standing from his desk to speak eye to eye. "Don't let them see you like this."

"Don't let them see me like this? Fuck, Stan, there are aliens in our office; how am I supposed to react?"

"Remain steady and relaxed," Stan answered calmly. "It's how I've avoided any trouble with them so far. From what I've gathered, they're planning a full-scale invasion of our planet. I've been in meetings with them, and it sounds like it's all going down at 1:00 tomorrow afternoon. But I've got a plan to stop it, Peter, and with your help, I believe it'll succeed. Just wait for my signal at noon tomorrow, then meet me in my office."

"What is it? What are you planning?"

"I'm sorry, Peter, I can't go into details right now. Already, I see some of them walking this way for our morning meeting. Just trust me on this; tomorrow at noon. But for now, act naturally. Don't let them suspect anything."

Peter nodded just as the first knock on the door interrupted any further conversation between the two. He turned and opened the door, allowing several others entrance, cautiously eyeing each of them as they shuffled past him. Before exiting, he glanced at Stan, who nodded in return and gave a subtle wink. Peter then walked out, leaving them to their "meeting."

He went to his desk and sat motionless for several minutes, trying to gather himself to maintain coherent thought. He couldn't believe what was happening, but he couldn't let on either. *"Act naturally,"* Stan told him, a near-impossible task after having just learned the truth about what had been going on. Still, his best chance at accomplishing that was to have as little interaction with others as possible. He thought about going home, but leaving early would most assuredly draw suspicion. Plus, he couldn't leave Stan by himself; he was the only one who knew the plan. If something were to happen to him, Peter wouldn't forgive himself, and all of Earth would be in danger of being invaded by the alien beings set to take over. No, he would stay as he had always done, sacrificing his own sanity for his work and his boss.

He often referred to it as the greater good, but it was the main reason his marriage deteriorated and why his wife eventually left him. This time, however, he wasn't sacrificing to build a better life for only the two of them, though it had always been his greatest wish. He was doing it for every person on the planet.

Burying his face in the various ledgers scattered about his desk, he focused on his work and set about correcting the grievous error earlier detected in his client's accounts. The stress and fear hadn't weighed so heavily on him that he couldn't overcome the slight inconvenience of an unbalanced report. He was still good at math, aliens or not.

Tirelessly working all day, ignoring all others around him, never leaving his desk except for the occasional trip to the bathroom, and even working through his lunch break, Peter managed to forget all about the strange behaviors of his coworkers until it was time to go home, and the harsh reality inevitably reared its ugly face.

Norm was the first to walk by, a crooked smile plastered on his face as he stared at Peter.

"Tomorrow, buddy." Then his head started bobbing persistently, a reminder he wasn't at all human.

Roger walked by next, just as Peter was gathering his things, his coworker's lips curled upward in that same unnatural smile.

"Tomorrow's the day, Peter. Can't wait." Then *his* head, too, began to bob uncontrollably.

As Peter stepped out of his cubicle, witnessing the others in the office scrambling for the elevator, their expressions mirroring each other, he saw Stan outside his office door, waving goodbye and smiling like the others. Only, when he locked eyes with Peter, he winked again and said, "Tomorrow, Peter." Then Peter walked away, opting to take the stairs.

Back in the small interrogation room, the officers were losing their patience and getting annoyed by Peter's story. He hadn't yet told them what they wanted to hear, though he'd been rambling for over an hour. The standing officer stepped forward, believing he could provoke Peter into letting something slip.

"Was it because your wife left you? Is that what this was about?"

"Peter shifted his eyes upward to the second officer, irritated at the man's insinuation.

"What?" Peter snapped angrily. "Why would you think that?"

"You mentioned your wife had left you a few months back. That can take its toll on someone. Do you want to know what I think? I think you got angry after your wife left you. I think you've had a hard time being on your own, the thought of her moving on with her life infuriating you until that pent-up rage needed escape."

"My wife leaving me had nothing to do with this," Peter raged through gritted teeth. "Leave her out of this."

"Then help us out here, Peter," the seated officer stated more calmly. "Help us to understand. What was it?"

"It…it was..,"

"Oh, for Christ's sake," the standing officer jumped in again, "tell us, already," as he slammed his palm on the table, causing Peter's body to jolt.

"IT WAS THE WINK!" Peter yelled. "Don't you see? He winked at me. Twice! If you knew anything about Stan at all, you'd know that wasn't him. He was pretending, like all the rest. He almost had me convinced he was human. But I saw through his lies."

"Here we go with the alien bullshit again," the angry officer said, throwing his hands in the air.

"I'm telling you the truth," Peter said loudly. "They were waiting for a signal from the skies. Probably from their mothership or something. It was going to happen at…" His voice dwindled as he glanced across the table at the officer's watch. "What time is it?"

The officer looked at his watch, then stared back at Peter. "It's 12:30," he responded. "Why? Do you think you're going somewhere?"

"It's happening at 1:00," Peter responded.

"What's happening at 1:00?"

"It's what I've been trying to tell you guys. I thought about it all night, not getting a minute of sleep. They couldn't fool me; not even Stan, with his story about having a plan to stop it. I mean, why was he even in the meetings with them to begin with unless he was one of them? It was all a ploy to make me believe he was one of us when he was really one of them. I think he was worried about me stopping them from carrying out their plan. And he was right to be worried. I couldn't let them get away with it. I had to do something. And that's when it came to me."

"What did you do, Peter?" the calmer of the two officers asked. "You can tell us. We just need to hear you say it."

"I did what I had to do."

Friday
The elevator up to the third floor seemed to last an eternity, which worked in his favor. It allowed him to control his breathing, to lessen the quivering in his hands. He couldn't stop what was coming, but he could send a warning that the human race would not be so easily put down without a fight. And those in the office of Hammond and Fincher - the aliens posing as humans – they couldn't stop what was coming either.

As the elevator doors slid open, Peter lifted the front of his shirt and pulled the pistol from his waistband. The first shot was delivered almost immediately, as Chuck happened to be walking by on his way to the bathroom. The bullet ripped into his chest, dropping him to the floor instantly. The gunshot caused many to stand from their desks in curiosity at the loud sound.

Evelyn's only mistake was that she sat in the nearest cubicle.

Her nearest neighbor, Gloria, had no time to react as blood sprayed across her face from the bullet exiting the side of Evelyn's head. That was when the screaming began, as panic swept through the office. Staff members dove under their desks, hoping not to be seen, while others darted from their cubicles, taking cover in the labyrinthine maze between the fabric walls of their offices.

Stan had witnessed the first kill from where he sat behind his desk and managed to run to his door and close it without being detected. He immediately called 911 to report the hostile shooting while listening to the awful sound of repeated gunshots as Peter made his way across the office floor.

One by one, Peter relentlessly stalked his prey, firing upon his coworkers, killing them where they hid. If any tried to run for the elevator, as a few had done, he'd shoot them in the back, uncaring of how he ended their lives. Gloria, Norm, Yusef, and even Roger, his closest friend in the office, were shot down in cold blood, victims of Peter's uncompromising assault. Eleven victims in all until only one remained.

Stan cowered behind his desk as his door was kicked open by the crazed assailant. He knew his life could be ending in seconds and chose to go out a whimpering lamb as he threw his hands up in front of his chest and dropped to his knees, pleading for his life.

"Please, Peter. Don't do this. I have a wife and two kids; they need me. If you let me live, I swear I won't tell them; I won't tell anyone it was you."

"Tell them?" Peter questioned rhetorically. "No, you won't tell *them*." The next shot fired was the one that ended Stan's life as his body slumped forward, blood trickling out of the hole in his forehead.

The two officers looked at each other, disgusted yet pleased at the confession they had just received from the unstable perpetrator. They were beginning to think they weren't going to break him before he demanded a lawyer. The standing officer signaled toward the door, where another officer outside entered.

"Take him to a holding cell; we got what we needed."

"What?" Peter cried as he was being dragged away. "Wait! Didn't you guys hear me? They weren't human. They were aliens. I probably saved lives by killing them. I saved lives!"

His voice faded into the distance, leaving the two officers alone in the small room.

"Fucking loony probably won't even do any real time," the one officer said. "You watch; Judge Nielewics will send him to the state hospital instead. He's too lenient on these twisted fucks. This fucking guy should get the chair. That was quite a crazy story he was telling though, huh? The sick bastard probably doesn't even realize today is April 1st, and his coworkers were just playing an April Fools prank on him."

"Hey, he's off the streets," the other officer pointed out. "That's what matters.

"Yeah, I suppose. What time you got? Want to grab some lunch? I'm starving."

The second officer looked at his watch again. "It's two minutes 'til one. And sure, but you're buying."

They walked out of the room, satisfied with their accomplishment.

Back in the office of Hammond and Fincher, the coroner and his forensics team were still combing through the wreckage of the morning's tragedy, where lifeless bodies were soaked in blood and strewn about the room's layout. Suddenly, one of the victims' cell phone lit up with a text message. Then another's lit up, and another's, and another's after that until eventually, all the cell phones were activated.

"Hey, a message just came through this guy's phone," one of the forensics staff blurted, bending over to read it. "It says, 'respond if safe for arrival.' What do you suppose that means?"

"This one over here says the same thing," a second voice called out.

"Yup, same here," came a third response.

"All of them," the coroner stated, sweeping from one phone to the next. "They all have the same message. "That is very strange. I have no idea what it means."

Across the distance of space, an alien warship that had readied its massive fleet for conquest receives no reply from their brothers. Speculating that their comrades must have fallen to the deadly species of Earth and concluding that humans must be a violent and brutal race of beings who will not be easily subjugated, they abandon their mission, choosing instead to chart a course to another galaxy in hopes of finding a less hostile planet in which to conquer.

4

Slug

"What do you suppose it is?" the skinny boy with the glasses queried. Charlie hadn't learned his name yet, but he was sure it was the boy's first time camping.

"I don't know," Charlie replied, eyeing the strange, gooey creature he found basking on a rock by the river, "but it's alive; I saw it move."

He reached for a small stick by his feet while the small group of children huddled closer to get a better look at the odd-looking organism he had found.

"Is it a leech?" Dennis yelled out from the back of the pack. "My mom always tells me to watch out for leeches when I jump in the river back home."

"It's not a leech, Dennis," Charlie replied. "Leeches are black, not red with yellow stripes."

He readied the stick for poking, wanting the other kids to see it move just as he had.

"I don't think that's a good idea," Kerry said. "Maybe you should just let it be."

"I'm not going to hurt it or anything," Charlie responded, "I'm just going to give it a little nudge."

"I still think it's wrong," she added. "It's probably just a poor snail that lost its shell or something."

Charlie turned and gave Kerry a confused and frustrated look. He wondered why she had even followed the small group of boys to the river. He would have told her to go back to the campsite, but he knew his mother would have his hide if he excluded his little sister, especially after how frightened she was after the earthquake two nights earlier. It had only been some mild tremors, certainly not as bad as a few other quakes California had seen over the years, but still enough to cause his sister anxiety.

"Have you ever even seen a snail?" he questioned.

"I saw it move!" the boy with the glasses stated excitedly, pointing at the odd thing to draw everyone's attention to it (as if they wouldn't have known where to look had his finger not been indicating).

In unison, everyone leaned in closer, focusing on the colorful, living globule, all mumbling as one.

"I don't see it moving."

"It's not now."

"Chip, move your hand; I can't see."

"Hey, stop pushing."

"Shhh! You'll scare it."

"This is stupid."

"Shut up, Timmy."

Charlie tuned out all the background noise, concentrating on the slug-like creature.

"Guys, guys...quiet!" he shouted. "Does anyone else hear that?"

"Hear what?" Dennis questioned.

"Shhh...listen."

Sssssssssss

"Did you hear it?" Charlie asked again, more excitedly the second time.

"I heard it," Walter said.

"Me too," Chip added. "It sounded like hissing."

"I didn't hear anything," Dennis stated disappointedly and with a hint of doubt in his voice.

"Well, listen already."

"I am, stupid."

"Yeah, you *are* stupid."

"I meant *you* were the stupid one."

"Shut up, dill hole."

Sssssssssssssssss

"There it is again," Kerry cried out. "I heard it."

"Yeah, me too."

"Did you hear it that time, Dennis?" Charlie inquired.

Dennis, wide-eyed, nodded his head feverishly.

"I told you it's alive," Charlie reiterated, a cocky smile adorning his face.

"But still," Timmy jumped in, "what is it? I've never seen anything like that, and my parents are always watching those nature and animal shows on the Discovery Channel."

"Oh yeah," Jacob said enthusiastically, "I *like* those. Did you see the one where the birds would do that funny dance to attract a mate?"

"Nobody cares about the bird episodes, Jacob," Dennis spoke up. "I watch the ones with the tribespeople. They sometimes show women's boobs."

"Eeeew!" Kerry squealed. "That's gross."

"You can't say those things in front of my sister," Charlie stated, giving his friend a dirty glance. "She'll run and tell our mom."

"I can't help that they're topless," Dennis said as he shrugged his shoulders.

Skkkssssssssskk

"Whoa!" Lucas exclaimed as the group shuffled back from the unusual red and yellow critter after it hissed more assertively. "Did you see that? It just spit something out of the front of its body."

"I didn't see it."

"Me neither."

"I missed it too."

"Well, you can see the green slime in front of it on the rock, can't you?" Lucas questioned, pointing at a moist blotch of olive green staining the rock's surface.

"I think that was already there," Chip chimed in.

"No, it wasn't," Lucas argued. "I watched it spit it out."

"Wait," Charlie interjected, "how do you know that's the front of the thing?"

"I told you; I saw it spit it out."

"I mean, what if that's the back? Maybe it just pooped it out."

"Oh right," Lucas answered. "I'm not touching that thing then."

"I don't think any of us should touch it," Kerry added.

"Shut up, Kerry," her brother chided. "You've been acting stupid since the earthquake."

"Oh, hey," Walter jumped in, "that was pretty cool the other night. Did anyone else feel it?"

"We did at our house," Jacob replied.

"Mine too," Dennis answered, raising his hand slightly as if he were in school.

"We had a picture fall off the wall at our house," Timmy joined in. "I wasn't scared though."

"Guys!" Charlie raised his voice. "Can we focus here? We're not talking about the earthquake; we're talking about this little guy." He pointed toward the colorful slime creature.

"I don't know, Charlie," Timmy started. "Maybe your sister's right; maybe you shouldn't touch it. What if you catch something from it?"

"You sound like a wuss, Timmy."

"So. At least I'm not going to get green poop on my hand."

"I'm with Timmy," Lucas said. "Can't we just stop bothering it?"

"We're not bothering it," Charlie responded. "We're just looking at it."

"You were going to poke it," Kerry said.

"I *was*," he said, "but I've changed my mind." He looked at the others, staring into each of their eyes, searching for a hint of bravery. When he found none, he opted to set his sights on the boy he didn't know, standing behind the others. Nodding to get the boy's attention, he called out, "You. What's your name?"

The boy looked to his left and his right, skeptical that it was to him Charlie had been talking.

"M-me?" he questioned, pressing his thumb to his chest.

"That's right," Charlie said. "What's your name?"

"I'm Chip," the boy responded

"You haven't camped here before, have you?"

"No, but Timmy's mom invited us."

"That's fine," Charlie continued, "but you see, we've all been coming here for years. You can't just show up here your first time, thinking you can join our group; you have to be initiated. Isn't that right, boys?"

Smirking and giggling, the other boys fell in line, turning their attention to the newcomer and nodding their heads in agreement.

"Yeah, that's right," Dennis concurred. "I almost forgot about that."

Kerry shook her head in puzzlement, "You guys never had an initiation before."

Charlie stared at his younger sister sternly. "Shut up, pipsqueak. Yes, we have. He's gotta do something to prove he's worthy."

"You're being stupid," Kerry stated, stomping off in the direction of the trail that had led them to the river bed. "And I'm telling mom you called me pipsqueak," she yelled back as she disappeared into the forest line.

"You're going to get in trouble now," Jacob stated.

"No, I'm not. My mom will have forgotten all about it by the time we get back. Now Chip," Charlie continued where he'd left off before his sister interrupted him, "do you want to be part of our group or not?"

"Wh-what do I have to do?"

"I'm going to relinquish this stick and allow you to be the one to poke that thing." He swung his arm toward the colorful ball of slime, pointing the small twig he held in his hand at the creature as if it were a magical wand.

"That's it?" Chip questioned. "That's all I gotta do; just poke it?"

Timmy grabbed the boy's sleeve, shaking his head, "You don't have to, Chip. Charlie's just joking."

Curling his upper lip, Charlie reeled back and punched Timmy in the shoulder. "I'm not joking, Timmy. He's gotta do it."

"Yeah!" Dennis stated, nodding his head.

"I think he *has* to," Walter agreed.

"And, if he doesn't," Charlie added, "then *you're* out of our group, too, since he's *your* friend."

Hearing that and looking at his friend with apologetic eyes, Chip held out his hand. "I'll do it."

Timmy released Chip's sleeve, dropped his head, and took a step back. Charlie smirked and handed over the splinter of driftwood he'd been holding. Chip wrapped his hand around it tightly, clutching it like a knife. He could feel his fingernails digging into his palm. Had he the will, he could have buried the wooden shank in Charlie's midsection; the thought had crossed his mind. But he was never one to stand up for himself or others. He had always been the meek little boy who let everyone walk all over him. Now was his chance to show the others that he wasn't afraid; he wasn't pathetic. If he did this one thing, they would see he was one of them; he would finally fit in with his peers.

Stepping forward, making sure his shoulder brushed against Charlie's chest, nudging the stubborn boy back a bit to flaunt his newly-found bravado, Chip leaned forward and stared at the striped slug, gathering his wits.

Ssssssssssss

The slimy thing hissed its warning, causing Chip to stand upright in apprehension.

"Look at him," Dennis started, "he's scared."

"He *looks* scared," Jacob agreed.

"I'm *not* scared," Chip argued, keeping his eyes fixed on the slimy critter. "It just hissed at me, is all."

"Then, what are you waiting for?" Charlie egged him on, "Go on and poke it."

Other voices joined in.

"Yeah, poke it."

"Just do it already."

"Chicken!"

"You *are* scared, ain't ya?"

SLUG | **53**

Chip looked back at Timmy standing behind the others, the boy's face showing sadness, offering that he, too, wasn't courageous enough to stand up against his friends. "Just get it over with, Chip," Timmy said softly, sullenly.

Biting his lower lip, Chip turned back to the red and yellow blob resting on the rock. He took a big gulp and extended his shaking hand toward the creature, ready to poke it and hoping it was as docile a thing as it had so far been portraying. Just as the point of the stick was about to prod the unusual organism, a loud, stern voice yelled out.

"Jacob, Lucas, what are you boys doing?"

Startled by the man's rough voice, Chip dropped the stick and straightened himself up, turning with the others toward the treeline to see from whom the voice belonged. Charlie and the other boys recognized the harsh tone instantly. It was Lucas and Jacob's father, a gruff outdoorsman with little tolerance for disobedience, especially from those who were in his immediate family.

"You better get your butts over here if you don't want them tanned."

"Yes, sir," the two boys said simultaneously, synchronized perfectly from years of practice. Lucas turned to his friends. "We've gotta go; see you back at the campsite."

As the two brothers strode across the rocky bank of the river's edge toward their waiting father with their heads hung in embarrassment, the man was looking beyond them at the five remaining stragglers, curious about their questionable activities.

"You other boys," he called out, "what no-good are you up to?"

Timmy and Chip remained silent, shaking their heads and shrugging their shoulders, while Dennis, Walter, and Charlie knew it wiser to communicate verbally.

"Nothing."

"Nothing, sir."

"Nothing, Mr. Freemont."

"You'd *better* be up to 'nothing,'" he shouted. "In fact, why don't you boys join us on our walk back? You shouldn't be out here horsing around anyway."

The five boys looked at each other, waiting for one among them to be the first to heed the man's request.

"Maybe you boys didn't hear me," Mr. Freemont reiterated louder. "Don't make me do something you boys will regret."

All at once, the boys' tense shoulders dropped in submission as they fell in line and slowly followed in the footsteps of their previously beckoned comrades, forgetting all about the colorful globule perched on the large rock behind them.

It's just as well. Some things are better left undisturbed. Such is the case with the brightly-colored slug that had acquired the children's attention. Its slumber had already been disturbed two nights earlier, when the ground quaked and opened a fissure, releasing the unique organism back into the world it had so long ago been separated from.

Its age was undeterminable, but it had existed since prehistoric times. For millions of years, it had been trapped in an underwater tomb, living on amoebas and other microscopic organisms and parasites that inhabited the tight space between layers in the Earth's crust; but it hadn't always been that way.

Back when giant lizards had roamed the vast landscape, claiming dominance over this world, these tiny creatures crash-landed here, reluctant passengers on a fragment of space rock that had fallen to Earth during a meteor shower.

At first, feeding on plankton and microfauna to sustain their otherworldly appetite, they slowly evolved to feast on the more solid inhabitants of their newly-adopted planet, such as the arthropods and cephalopods of that long-ago era.

Soon, even the two and four-legged behemoth kings of the land became meals to the alien slugs from space. Their malleable bodies excrete a viral enzyme that is absorbed into a host's skin upon contact, contaminating that which it touches with an infectious disease that slowly breaks down the biological functions of living creatures until they wither away and die, allowing for easier consumption by the slugs.

The disease delivered upon the ancient lizards had propagated like a plague, transmitting the contagious enzyme from beast to beast upon the slightest touch of their leathery skin.

In time, gigantic bodies littered the harsh geographic terrain, providing sustenance for the invasive species, driving the dinosaurs to near-extinction before an asteroid smashed into the Earth, finishing the job that the striped slugs had started. The asteroid would shoulder the blame for the dinosaurs' demise, but in truth, they were already an endangered species by the time the large rock devastated the global environment.

Years later, when the dust and ash had settled, the extra-terrestrial slugs had perished along with their prey, save for one of their kind, buried under dirt and clay, finding itself trapped in a sedimentary womb.

Now, after the other night's earthquake had reopened a fissure in the hardened soil, it has crawled up from its earthen prison, patiently waiting for another food source upon which to feed. And it may not have long to wait.

From out of the treeline where the trail from the campsite opened to the rocky riverbed, a young boy emerged. He hadn't come on this camping trip to be ridiculed and made fun of. He had been used to that treatment back home. But here, amongst a new group of friends, he could be something more; he could show them he was brave.

Defying his mother's wishes once he had returned to camp, Chip ran back down the trail that led to the river. He was in search of the slug that the others had asked him to poke. He wasn't going to back down; he would show them.

As he approached the rock with the basking slug, he noticed the stick he had dropped earlier and disregarded its usefulness. Just poking the odd-looking thing wouldn't be enough; the others wouldn't believe he had done it. Instead, he would bring the odd creature back with him to show the others how much he wanted to be a part of their group. And as Chip reached for the slimy organism, the colorful slug hissed with delight.

Sssssssssss

5

Safe at Home

The glow from his flashlight barely pierced the blackness of the darkened room. He couldn't turn the lights on and risk someone outside noticing. Perhaps nobody would care, but he couldn't take the chance. He had worked too hard, planned for too long, to have it all come crashing down before his eyes when he was finally so close.

He had spent weeks casing the property, surveilling the staff, those that remained, anyway, the most loyal to the Manzini family. He had learned all of their schedules, taking meticulous notes of their arrival and departure times. They never strayed from their previously arranged timetables. That was how he knew *this* was the safest time to enter, when nobody would be around for the next several hours.

He was comfortable in his trade, never letting down a client who had hired him for his unique talent. This job would be no exception. He felt a smirk overtake his face as his thoughts wandered back to his first meeting with his client and her unusual request.

"You *do* understand what I am asking you, Mr. Franco, do you not?" she questioned after his dismissive response.

"Oh, I heard you, Mrs. Manzini."

"It's *Ms.* Manzini, Mr. Franco, and I don't appreciate your arrogant demeanor."

"With all due respect…," he paused for effect, "*Ms.* Manzini…," emphasizing the 'Ms.' to make a point, "you wanted the best, that's why you contacted me. You don't have to like my demeanor to know I'll get the job done."

She glanced at him with a sideways stare, taking another drag from her long-stem, opera-style cigarette holder. The man was a self-absorbed, condescending lout, but she could tolerate his cockiness if he were able to deliver that which she coveted.

"Very well, Mr. Franco. The agreement is half now, and the other half when you've delivered the package to me. Is that clear?"

She reached for the shoebox that sat beside her on the sofa and placed it on the ornate coffee table in front of her, slowly sliding the box forward toward him.

Leaning sideways in his chair with his arms folded about his chest, he glanced down at the box, then shifted his eyes back up to meet hers. He crinkled his nose, then reached up with his thumb to swipe across the mustache that adorned his upper lip as if tending to a slight tickle. He then tucked his hand back into the gap between his bicep and chest, resuming his position, before tilting his head and shifting his gaze first to his right, then to his left to gather information about his surroundings.

"You have a pretty nice place here, Ms. Manzini. You look like you're doing well for yourself. If you don't mind me asking..."

"I *do* mind, Mr. Franco," she cut him off. "You are here merely for a business proposition, not idle chit-chat. Twenty thousand was the offer; ten now, ten more when the item is in my possession. Do we have an understanding?"

He smirked and nodded, respecting her wishes of not wanting to discuss personal matters. He reached for the small box as she continued.

"It's all there, Mr. Franco; no need to count it."

"Oh, I have no doubt it's the proper amount, Ms. Manzini. I don't make a habit of distrusting my clients. If they cheat me, it always comes back on them. Unfavorably, I might add." He followed up his comment with a devious grin.

The woman's expression grew concerned as she swallowed heavily before drawing in a deep breath.

"Yes, well, I trust you can get this matter promptly taken care of, Mr. Franco?"

"It's a big house," he responded, "with a lot of people coming and going; I'll need some time, but yes, I can get it done for you."

"You have two months, Mr. Franco. It must be in my possession before then. It is imperative."

"It is imperative," he whispered to himself, mocking his client as he looked around the dimly lit room, the narrow beam from his flashlight only offering brief glimpses of the wonderment within. Though Ms. Manzini had acted snobbish and grand, he knew the real story. He always did his research before taking on new clients.

As it turned out, Ms. Manzini's husband was the one with all the money, at one point, earning millions in endorsements as he traveled across the country, performing in front of thousands while perfecting his craft. But like so many others who let fame and fortune go to their heads, he thought he was above reproach. When the media found out about the scandalous affair he was having with his assistant, they tore him down, piece by piece, eventually leaving his career in shambles.

After their divorce, Ms. Manzini moved into the couple's second home, which she had been awarded, along with a cash settlement of nine hundred and fifty thousand dollars. It was a far cry from her husband's net worth, but he had the best divorce attorney money could buy and therefore retained most of his wealth.

Still, she made out all right. Her settlement was enough money for most people to live on for the rest of their lives, but Ms. Manzini spent above her means, squandering cash on lavish jewelry and fine antiquities. In only five years, she was broke, except for a small amount of savings she held onto for emergencies. Mr. Franco figured this must be what was classified as an emergency in her mind.

Panning the light across the different articles displayed around the darkened room, he shook his head in awe. The study, which he now found himself in, was impeccably furnished, the style befitting that of royalty. Lining each wall, display cases filled with extravagant and luxurious pieces, gathered from every corner of the globe, sat undisturbed, flaunting their owner's wealth. On the walls, amidst various priceless paintings that any serious collector would drool over, hung the retired objects of the owner's trade. From different ropes to chains to steel shackles, they draped from large wooden pegs located between each of the framed pieces of artwork. Toward one corner, built into the wall, was an eight-foot-wide glass wardrobe. Within the enclosure, six colorful capes, worn by the owner throughout his career, hung at attention as if saluting all who entered the room. Across from the vibrant adornments, on the far wall, a large self-portrait of the man himself, Manfred Manzini, more commonly known to the public as "Manzini the Magnificent, Escape Artist Extraordinaire."

During his research, Mr. Franco had read that after Manzini the Magnificent's fall from grace, he would often disappear for months at a time, traveling to Asia to seek guidance and wisdom from Nepali and Tibetan monks. There were even whispers that the disgraced man had been honing his skills, learning to escape from more elaborate entrapments, and preparing himself to make a return to prominence. But all of those rumors seemed to fade when he disappeared over a year ago, never returning. Only his staff remained faithful and hopeful of his return, continuing their duties and maintaining the property. And why not; they were still getting paid to do so, receiving automatic deposits into their accounts.

None of that mattered to Mr. Franco at the moment; his eyes focused on the prize situated just below the self-portrait of the famed escape artist. It was the object for which he had been hired.

Mr. Franco was a cat burglar, priding himself on being able to break into just about anywhere to steal just about any*thing*, but his real expertise was in safecracking. And standing before him, in all its glory, was the most beautiful steel vault he had ever seen.

It was a Deitrich-Heigu Triple-combination Slingsteader, the most difficult personal safe to crack. It stood five and a half feet tall, twenty-four inches wide, and nineteen inches deep. It was gloss black with the letters D-H inlaid in gold on the front and had three chrome-plated dial combinations just to the left of the door lever. He had only ever seen one other of its kind, but he still managed to break into it in under three hours. This one looked more intimidating, but he had every intention of beating his record.

He imagined Manfred must have stashed a few million dollars within if the man's ex-wife was willing to drain her own account to get her hands on it. Then the thoughts started swirling in his head. He had never cheated or let down a client, but he had never had a job with such a take before. If there *were* millions inside, Ms. Manzini would certainly have no clue about the amount. It would be easy to skim fifty thousand off the top without anyone being the wiser. But he was a professional and quickly dismissed the idea. The first rule of hired thievery: you don't scam your clients. They'll always find out, and you'll soon be dead.

He shuffled over to the far wall, slinking past the furniture and keeping the beam of light focused on the black beauty. He could feel himself getting anxious as he moved closer to it, the thought of breaking into a Deitrich-Heigu a second time overwhelming his senses.

First, he visually inspected its outer casing for any trips or alarms. Some people were extra cautious like that, although installing such devices on a D-H was unnecessary; he knew of only three people in the world who could crack one, and he was among the three. After determining the safe was clear of any external contraptions that could alert the staff or authorities, he let out a slow, steady breath as he placed his gloved hand on the top of the safe and slid it from one side to the other, taking in the feel of the smooth, hard surface. He then rubbed his fingers over the marvelously detailed gold letters shown across the front, displaying the initials of the two gentlemen who designed such a superbly crafted device: Franz Deitrich and Kenji Heigu, an exquisite pairing of brilliant German and Japanese engineers. Letting his fingers glide down from the gold embellishments, he traced around the three dials that formed an equilateral triangle: two on the right and one centered between them on the left. It was a fine work of artistry, but he couldn't let himself get caught up in the moment; he had a job to do.

He glanced at his watch and realized he'd taken a bit longer admiring the safe and the other incredible items within the study than he had anticipated. In the business of safecracking, every minute counted. He now had two hours and forty-two minutes before the first staff member made their unwelcomed arrival. He had left himself no choice but to beat his personal best.

Getting on his knees, he pressed his right ear to the cold, steel face of the door just below the dials. Reaching over his head, he caressed the top dial between his fingers and began methodically turning it to the left until he heard the faint clicking sound of the first tumblers disengaging. The first number on the first dial was always the easiest on the D-H Slingsteader. After that, things got complicated. Each of the dials had a different combination, and each of the dials' tumblers had to release one number at a time. It's what made this vault's internal, sophisticated mechanisms the marvel of safe designers everywhere. The problem was, though it's perfect in its design, it was impractical for everyday use, which is why the D-H was never mass-produced, and there has never been another design like it since. There were only eleven of them ever manufactured, and only eight ever sold.

He pulled a notepad from his pants pocket and jotted the first number, 62, at the top of the page. It was the first hurdle but not much of one; the top dial was always the first number. Now, he had to decide which dial was next. Every D-H Triple-combination Slingsteader was made unique. The order in which the dials are turned is critical in opening the safe. If the wrong dial is chosen in any sequence of three, releasing its tumbler would then relock every previous one, forcing you to start over.

In a time crunch, he decided to forego using the eeny, meeny, miny, moe method, instead immediately snatching the dial on the left. It was a fifty-fifty shot; no sense taking the time.

Placing his ear to the door once again, he turned the second dial, listening for the familiar clinking sound of the tumbler disengaging. Once he heard it, his eyes opened wide, surprised at the result. If he had guessed wrong on the second dial, the subtle clinking sound would have been followed by a louder clanking noise, signifying the first dial's tumbler re-engaging. He heard no such sound as he let out a breath of relief. He had guessed correctly. Writing 37 in his notepad, he now knew the lower dial was the next to tackle.

A few minutes later, he had the first set of tumblers released, and he was ready to move on to the second sequence of numbers. It was a crucial decision he had to make; which dial to start with now? He glanced at his watch, keeping track of the time. Two hours and twenty-seven minutes remaining. It only took him fifteen minutes to figure out the first three numbers. Not bad, he thought, but the fun was only beginning. Should he guess wrong on any subsequent choices, which he was bound to do, all his previous efforts would be lost, and he would have to start again.

There were 214 possible dial choices to make after the first dial. The good news was, after the first round of three, the number dropped significantly to 36. Since the first three numbers were now known: 62, 37, and 45, it was now a game of trial and error, with time quickly ticking away with every wrong choice made. He took a deep breath, grabbed the first dial between his thumb and forefinger, and leaned in to begin the tedious work of solving the puzzle.

It was a skill, listening for the inner mechanisms to do their dance while keeping his breathing in check. Any exterior sounds or a loss of concentration could keep him from hearing the crucial sound of the gears as the tumbler released. He was up for the challenge as his fingers methodically rotated the first dial to the right, passing each incremental marking at a snail's pace, hoping he had chosen wisely.

An hour and six minutes later, and a notebook page filled with scribbled out notes from the sequence mistakes he'd made (mistakes that had forced him to start over four times), he had solved the second series of numbers. He had one more sequence of three, six more possible dial choices standing in his way, and an hour and twenty-one minutes to accomplish the feat. As far as he was concerned, the safe was as good as cracked.

Getting right to it, he wiped his forearm across his brow, removing the sweat that had accumulated, and reached for the lowest dial to begin the last series of what was purely guesswork.

It took him three tries and forty-two minutes to guess the correct dial, eating away valuable time, which was bound to happen. He made up for it on the second dial, which he chose correctly on his first attempt, leaving just the one. He took a final deep breath and began spinning the last dial ever so carefully, listening for the beautiful sound of..,

Clink!

He opened his eyes and pulled his head away from the door, his heart beating faster in his chest. He had just done it; that was the last number. He turned his eyes to the dial, almost surprised that he had beaten a D-H Triple-combination Slingsteader a second time. He smiled and looked at his watch to see that another ten minutes had swiftly vanished. Still, he had just bested a nearly-impossible vault in only two hours and twenty-three minutes, leaving him just over ten minutes to clean out the safe and quickly disappear before the first worker arrived.

Reaching for the handle with an almost trembling in his hand, he pulled the lever down, feeling the steel rod unlock as it slid from its housing. He then reached into his duffel bag and pulled out three thin magnetic strips of differing lengths, each measuring a half-inch wide and about the same thickness as a popsicle stick.

One at a time, he slid the strips into the gap between the door and the safe wall, stacking them edge-to-edge until they were the full length of the door, creating an electromagnetic barrier in case of an internal alarm.

With the necessary precautions in place, he yanked on the handle, opening the bulky steel door, but what should have been an exciting moment, one he had been envisioning for over a month, was instead anticlimactic as he let out a heavy sigh while shaking his head in disappointment. His eyes, which had at first focused their stare on the lower section of the safe, then shifted to the shelf three-quarters of the way up that had a single piece of paper upon it. He pulled out the paper, read it, then placed it back on the shelf. With no alarm present, he then removed the magnetic strips from the metal frame, placed them into his bag, and slowly closed the door, contemplating how his next course of action would play out.

He quickly and stealthily left the premises undetected, nothing disturbed, and nobody the wiser that anyone had ever been inside. He was a professional, a master at his trade; leaving empty-handed wasn't something he was used to. And more, without the expected prize in hand to deliver to his client, he would be returning the ten thousand dollars to her. He could certainly keep some of it for his troubles, per the agreement they had struck, but he knew she would be needing it more than he, especially with her spending habits the way they were. It was all fine and well. The satisfaction of breaking into a D-H was rewarding enough for him.

As he made his way back to Ms. Manzini to refund her money and deliver the unfortunate news, he pondered the note within the safe. He wouldn't tell her about it; she didn't need to know. He wished *he* didn't know, but it was now his burden to bear.

The rumors were true, Manzini the Magnificent *was* honing his craft to make a comeback, but as it turned out, he wouldn't be coming back at all; the note was a goodbye of sorts, in case anything went wrong. And something *did*.

His greatest feat, the last performance Manfred attempted, which would have catapulted him back into the spotlight once again, was to escape his very own D-H Triple-combination Slingsteader. He must have passed away less than two weeks into his attempt. His corpse had been contorted in the lower half of the safe for over a year, long enough to fully decompose, leaving only his skeletal remains and the outline of a long-dried stain from when his body had once liquefied. It was an unsettling end to an incredible traveling escape artist who would now and forever remain safe at home.

6

Hide in Plain Sight

I understand why she loves to play this game. I always loved it as a child myself. The mystery, the running around, the feeling of suspense as you peek around every corner, looking for your target. It's a fun children's game without there ever being a true winner or loser - just a sense of accomplishment if you're the one seeking, and you find your target, or if you're the one hiding, and you can't be found. Nobody ever gets hurt, and everybody finishes with a smile. I was so glad when my little girl had gotten a new friend to play with.

We live in a little duplex apartment on Sterling, units 14A and 14B. Ours is unit 14B. The previous tenants in 14A had left a few months back, and Charlotte had been awfully lonely after that. She and the Rogers girl, Beverly, had become quite close. They would play together every day. When we heard the news about Dennis, Beverly's father, getting a promotion at work but that it would require the family to relocate to Chicago, Charlotte was heartbroken. She didn't have any other friends her age that she could play with, and I spent weeks consoling her.

Two weeks ago, Mr. Hanfrey, our landlord, found some new tenants to take the Rogers' place, and as luck would have it, they had a little girl my daughter's age. Charlotte was so excited that she went right over there and introduced herself to the little girl. Kids can be so funny. Mary is her name, short for Marilyn (her mother Pat is a huge Marilyn Monroe buff).

Pat and Chris just moved back to the area a month ago. They had been staying at his parent's house across town until they were able to find an affordable place closer to Mary's school. Charlotte and I were glad they took Mr. Hanfrey up on his offer.

It's been two weeks, and the girls have had a great time together. Pat's been wonderful to my little girl, letting her go over and play with Mary after school until dinner time. Well, she *had* been wonderful to Charlotte, that is, until yesterday.

I still don't understand what changed. Charlotte and Mary were playing Hide-and-Seek like they often did, and the next thing I know, Pat is yelling at Charlotte to get out. I ran out onto our shared porch and called to Charlotte, wondering what was going on.

Charlotte came running out to me, tears in her eyes, whimpering about the things Mary's mother was saying about her. I couldn't believe what I was hearing. If what Charlotte said was true, and I have no reason to think she would make something like that up, then Pat had some explaining to do. From what Charlotte told me, things got a little strange.

It was right at dinner time, and Pat had called upstairs to where the girls were playing to let Mary know it was time to eat. Mary yelled back that she hadn't found Charlotte yet. That was when Pat got a little upset and raised her voice.

"Is that so, young lady? You will tell your little friend she has to go, and you will come down here right now."

"But Mom, we were just.."

"No 'but's, Mary; I mean it. You've been playing all week long. If you don't tell your friend to go, I will."

It's one thing to speak to your own child like that, I know I've raised my voice to Charlotte on more than one occasion, but then she started yelling at my child, which is not ok with me.

"Charlotte, it's time for you to leave. Mary has to eat dinner. Do you hear me? I'm going to need you to get out, please."

At least she said "please." But then things became more heated.

"Mary, you need to come down to eat. Is your friend listening to me? Is she coming out?"

My Charlotte has always been good at hiding, and where she was, she could see Mary even though Mary couldn't see her. After Pat had asked the question, Mary stood at the top of the stairs, shaking her head. I understand Charlotte's not innocent in all this; she should have come out when Pat first called up to the girls, but they're only children, for crying out loud. They were only playing; it didn't give Pat the right to take her frustrations out on them. She charged upstairs and grabbed Mary by the wrist.

"Charlotte won't leave? That's it, then. When she does go, I don't want her coming back."

She pulled Mary by the wrist, forcing her down the stairs while looking back into the seemingly empty hallway and raising her voice.

"You hear that, Charlotte? I know you can hear me! I want you out of here, and I don't want you coming back! I don't want you playing with my daughter anymore!"

That was when I first heard the commotion and started making my way to the door. It was also when I heard Chris chime in.

"I knew this was going to happen. I told you from the start, Pat, she shouldn't have been playing with her little friend; it's only going to cause problems."

Cause problems? It only became a problem once they decided they didn't want *my* daughter playing with *their* daughter anymore. And now look what it's caused. I never wanted it to come to this, but they left me no choice.

After wiping away Charlotte's tears and telling her to go into the house and wait for me, I decided to have it out with the married couple. I didn't wait for anyone to open the door; I just barged right in on them getting ready to eat dinner. Mary was the first to notice me, and she could see how upset I was. She screamed and ran into the other room, her mother chasing behind her. Chris just sat in his chair with a smug look on his face like he didn't care why I was there. His shit-eating grin reeked of arrogance as if punishing my little girl was part of some master plan.

I suppose I could have handled things differently, perhaps had a calm conversation with the man, explaining how things looked from my point of view, but the knife was right there on the table, practically begging for me to pick it up.

I rarely lose my temper, but there was just something about that cocky smirk of his that caused my blood to boil. His look changed very quickly once I picked up the knife and plunged it deep into his chest.

"Not so full of yourself now, are you?" I said as I twisted the knife, watching the life slowly fade from his eyes. I give the man some credit; he didn't make so much as a peep during the whole dying process. When I pulled out the knife, his body slumped sideways, knocking over his chair and the chair next to his, as he plummeted to the floor in a heap. I wished it hadn't made as much noise as it had; it would have made my job easier. Instead, Pat came stumbling in on the scene, saw Chris staining the carpeted floor by the plasma spilling from his corpse, and screamed her head off, running back to shelter Mary from the sight (and, I suppose, also from me).

Chris was the first to fall, but I wasn't through yet. I wasn't going to harm Mary; she was an innocent child, but Pat had to pay for speaking to my child the way she had. And pay, she would.

So, here we find ourselves playing a similar game to what our daughters were playing just a short time earlier. As I said, I understand why Charlotte loves to play this game. The mystery, the running around, the feeling of suspense as you peek around every corner, looking for your target. It's exhilarating.

"Come out, come out, wherever you are."

I felt a smile invade my face as I gripped the knife tighter in my fist. I listened for any subtle movement as I slank from the dining room into the kitchen, my eyes shifting wildly from side to side, hoping to catch a glimpse of an awkward shadow that didn't belong. I quickly opened the pantry door, expecting to startle my helpless prey within, but only managed to frighten shelves stocked with canned vegetables and half-empty boxes of sugar-coated cereals.

"You can't hide for long. I'm going to find you."

"Why are you doing this?" a voice shouted from upstairs. *"What do you want from us?"*

She's not the best at this game; she just gave away her position. Still, there's a lot of ground to cover up there; maybe she'd surprise me.

With each step I took on my way up the stairs, I couldn't help but wonder if Pat was as excited about this experience as I was. I mean, the feeling of hiding out, maybe even in a cramped space, wondering if you're about to be found or if you'll live to play another day, it must be incredibly thrilling. I bet her heart is racing.

At the top of the stairs, I stopped and listened for heavy breathing. I heard nothing. But as I took a few more steps in the direction of the bedroom at the end of the hall, I heard the soft whispering.

"Yes, please hurry. There's someone in my house trying to kill us. My husband is already hurt; he's bleeding."

Hurt? Oh, honey, he's dead. As you soon would be. Calling 911 isn't going to save you.

"It's my daughter and me. We're hiding right now, but please hurry."

I could almost hear the trembling in her voice even at such a silent level. Just as I stepped through the threshold of the bedroom doorway, I heard the slight hint of muffled sobbing coming from behind the closed closet door. It's somewhat cliché, hiding in that location. I almost feel sorry that Pat's made it so easy for me. Maybe she should have been taking lessons from my daughter when our girls spent time playing this game. It's too late now.

I stepped in front of the closet door and paused, taking my time and building the suspense. I knew Pat must've seen the shadows of my shoes sneaking under the small opening at the base of the slatted door. What must be going on in her head right now? *Is she going to open it? Is she not going to open it? Will she? Won't she?* It must be killing her. I hope it doesn't; I want that pleasure.

"Ready or not, here I come," I teased. I had to; it's part of the game's charm. Reaching for the knob of the door with one hand and readying the knife in the other, I twisted and yanked the door open. Cowering in the corner was Pat, still holding the cellphone in her hand, the line still active as I heard the 911 operator's voice trying to calm what was about to be my next victim. Little sobbing Mary was on her knees behind her mother, gripping the back of Pat's pant legs like she was on a roller coaster ride. Only, this ride was about to come to an end.

"Please don't hurt my little girl!" Pat screamed.

What does she think I am, some horrible monster? That's ridiculous; I would never do such a thing.

Brandishing the knife threateningly so Pat wouldn't try anything stupid, I grabbed her wrist and yanked her from the closet, similar to how Charlotte told me she witnessed Pat yank Mary from the top of the staircase. Mary began to scream in terror. She's a smart kid; she knew what was coming next. I wouldn't let her be a witness to it, though. As I said, I'm not a monster.

"Get out of here, Mary!" I shouted. "Run to Charlotte next door."

She heard me loud and clear and bolted for the door as quickly as her legs could carry her, unrelenting tears streaming down her face. I felt sorry for the kid, but not as sorry as her mother was going to feel. I shoved Pat backward onto the bed and leaned over her, my empty hand clutching her throat. As I raised the knife overhead, and Pat began to struggle in my grasp, I stared into her eyes and noticed the realization had suddenly come to her. Some might think it was the look of knowing she was never going to see her little girl again, but I knew the truth. She now understood it was wrong to treat both of our daughters with such cruelty. It's too bad the realization came too late. I thrust the blade deep into her abdomen. She tried to scream but couldn't; my tight grip around her neck was cutting off her air supply. I'm not without compassion; I didn't want her suffering in pain. It's better that I end it quickly. I pulled the knife from her stomach and stabbed it into her a second time. Her struggling waned, and I released her throat just as blood shot from her mouth, causing her to gag on it. Seconds later, she expired.

My work was complete. I stood from Pat's dead body, leaving the knife embedded in her flesh, and calmly walked from the bedroom. As I made my way down the stairs, I reflected on my earlier thoughts. It was a mistake to think that what we were doing was only playing a fun children's game without there ever being a true winner or loser. Clearly, there was a loser. And the idea that nobody ever gets hurt, and everybody finishes with a smile; I guess that's not true either.

As I walked through the front door to head back to my side of the apartment duplex to check on Mary and Charlotte, I heard the distant screaming of sirens echoing through the still air. That's when the sudden awareness hit me.

The police would find Chris and Pat's dead bodies next door. They'd take Mary away and place her in a foster home, and my Charlotte would be left with nobody to play with again. I can't stand the thought of my daughter losing another friend. I won't let that happen.

It saddens me to think of all the friends my little girl has lost over the past forty-seven years. It's not her fault the parents can never see her. She never gained the ability to show herself physically as I have (although I only do it when absolutely necessary). So now, only the children ever see her. It's why she's so good at playing Hide and Seek.

I didn't want it to come to this, but now I know what I must do. There will be a third life I must take this day. I stepped through the door of apartment 14B, knowing that once I have killed the sweet, innocent Mary, my daughter will have a friend to play with for all eternity. That thought made me smile. And who knows, maybe the next tenants Mr. Hanfrey finds to fill apartment 14A will also have a little child. Then, the girls will have another friend they can spend their days playing with, having lots of fun, hiding in plain sight.

7

Night Wind

Danica always loved contemporary houses like the one she found herself in this evening. They had such rich character with their vaulted ceilings and unusual layouts. She admired the architecture of how they were made, every square inch utilized in one way or another, whether it be a crawl space at the back of a closet or additional storage areas tucked away behind hidden doorways under the staircase leading to the second floor. She loved how the living room's floor-to-ceiling windows bared all to nature and how, in return, nature opened up to her as she gazed out into the backyard. It was very comforting to her.

The Shonelys were new clients. She had previously babysat in this neighborhood a handful of times but never had the pleasure of babysitting for *this* couple's child. She was excited that her name was starting to make its way into the lives of those people, such as the Shonelys, who were considered among the elite; those figures whose paychecks were enough to have them labeled as members of "high society."

Both adult members of the household were doctors: specialists in their respective (and respected) fields. Derek Shonely was a Neurosurgeon, and his wife, Alicia, an Oncologist. Neither had qualms about flaunting their money to the rest of the neighborhood, as parked in the driveway were his-and-hers matching BMW X6s on display for all to gawk. The vehicles resided in the driveway because the garage was already housing another pair of the couple's toys: a Porsche 911 for him and an Audi SQ7 for her. Their home, too, displayed elements of their wealth, certain accouterments that spoke of both elegance and snobbish narcissism. None of that mattered to Danica. She was there now, in their home. In her mind, she now had the same level of importance in her job as they had in theirs. It could open new doors for her if she played her cards right. After all, they *hired* her to look after their son.

Benjamin Shonely, twelve years old, an only child, was the heir-apparent to the Shonelys' growing legacy of wealth. He had had everything handed to him since birth and was quite fond of getting his way with just about everything he asked. That was until the day before when his parents grounded him for his role in a recently uploaded video to a social media site depicting Benjamin and several of his friends bullying a young foreign exchange student. Benjamin's grounding was less about what he and his friends had done to the poor student but more about how it made the Shonelys look in the eyes of their peers. It was disgraceful to think that their son could tarnish their good names in such a fashion. Today was day two of five that he was serving in solitude in his bedroom.

Danica was a seasoned babysitter, able to handle even the most troublesome of children, but she was thankful Benjamin's punishment was imposed the day before, allowing him the opportunity to experience being "trapped" inside and under house arrest for already a day before she signed on to the job. She imagined his frustration level had probably diminished since his parents first broke the unfortunate news to him. She was about to find out as, with the stomping sound of footsteps echoing through the open foyer, the Shonelys marched down the grand staircase on their way to introduce their son to his new babysitter for the first time.

Benjamin was poised between his parents as they made their way down the stairs, the father's hand positioned firmly on the boy's shoulder as if preventing him from scampering off. Danica could see the scowl on the child's face and realized Derek was rightly warranted in holding the boy in his stanch grip; Benjamin would have done that very thing.

Arriving at the base of the staircase, Alicia was the first to speak as she shuffled sideways to present her dear baby boy.

"This is our son, Benjamin," she announced, exhibiting a smile. "Benjamin, this is Danica; she'll be your babysitter for tonight."

The boy just curled his lip in disgust and crossed his arms about his chest.

"Hi, Benjamin," Danica stated while waving her hand enthusiastically, hoping to ease a smile from the boy's lips. Benjamin turned his head away in silent defiance, choosing to continue his grimace even in the face of joyful exuberance.

"Can I go now?" the boy questioned in a harsh tone.

"Danica said 'Hi' to you," Derek replied, squeezing the boy's shoulder with his fingers. "The proper response is, 'Hello.'"

Danica noticed a slight wince interrupt Benjamin's frown as he turned his stare toward her.

"Hello," he grumbled, fighting back the urge to shout for fear he'd get more than just finger bruises adorning his shoulder if he had. "*Now*, can I go?"

"Oh, Derek," Alicia jumped in, "let the boy go back to his room. He's clearly still upset about his punishment and would rather be alone right now."

Derek tightened his lips and shook his head before rolling his eyes and releasing the boy, at which point, Benjamin spared no time darting back up the stairs. A few seconds later, the sound of a slamming door reverberated through the house. Alicia sighed and faked a smile as she turned to Danica.

"I'm sorry about that; he's upset because he and his friends had plans to hang out at Sphinx Arcade tonight, and well, *that's* not happening. I'm sure he'll be fine once he calms his head."

"I'm sure he will," Danica responded with a smile. "And please, no need to apologize."

"Thank you, Danica," Alicia replied before turning to her husband. "Derek, we should be off; we wouldn't want to be late. It'd be dreadful if we arrived after the Wallaces."

"Yes, dear," Derek replied. "Let me fetch our coats."

As he walked away to gather their things, Alicia continued her banter with Danica.

"Now, the boy's already eaten, so there's no need to fuss over him. I'm sure he'll spend most of the evening in his room playing his video games, anyway, but if he wants a snack, there's some microwave popcorn in the pantry. I hate even buying the stuff; it's like food for poor people, but he enjoys it. I can imagine you've had your share of that type of food, as well, so please, feel free to help yourself."

Danica's smile faded in favor of a subtle, agitated sneer at the woman's comment, which she was sure was an insinuation about her status of not being among the wealthy mucky-mucks of the city. Just then, Derek returned with their jackets slung over his arm, causing a half-hearted smile to return to Danica's face.

"Let's get going, dear," he said as he opened up his wife's jacket for her to slip her arms into, "the gala won't wait for us. As you said, we mustn't be late."

The Colonial Gala was a yearly gathering of the city's high-brow residents, where like-wealthy people could mingle among their own kind, disseminating tales of their fortunes and fame while sucking down glasses of overpriced champagne. Danica cared little for such nonsensical drivel but wasn't above caring for their children if it earned her some decent cash. She knew she could charge more when dealing with a family of such wealth.

"Our cell phones won't be on this evening," Alicia stated while walking toward the door, "but the number to The Shawnessy is on the sideboard in the dining room if you need to reach us. *Do* use the number sparingly, if at all possible," she added. "It would be very troubling to be disturbed at such an event and could reflect negatively on your compensation."

"What my wife is trying to express is, extreme emergencies only, please."

Danica nodded. "Got it," she said while holding back what it was she *really* wanted to say. "Don't worry about a thing; we'll be fine. Have yourselves a wonderful evening." Then the couple exited, and Danica closed the door behind them, pressing her back against the hardwood of its surface while rolling her eyes.

"Let us be off, dear," Danica murmured to herself, mocking the snooty couple, *"We mustn't be late to sniff the rich asses of our peers."* She snickered, "Give me a break."

Feeling a little less uptight once the couple had departed, Danica slowly wandered about the first floor, exploring the layout of the house. Several times, she found herself taking a detour through the living room so she could gaze out the expansive windows leading to the back deck and the beautifully landscaped yard beyond. Even now, though, with the sun beginning to set, the view was slowly fading, being replaced with the ever-sharpening image of her own reflection.

Stepping into the dining room, she noticed the card resting on the sideboard, as Alicia had mentioned, displaying the name and number of the hotel hosting the special event. The Shawnessy Hotel was *this* city's version of the Ritz Carlton. It was a hotel that she would never have the opportunity of staying in, with its pricey $500 per night rooms, but for tonight, she could imagine what it was like while she relaxed in the exquisite surroundings of the Shonelys' lavish home.

One disturbing element Danica noticed while surveying the couple's home was the lack of pictures of them together with their son. There were numerous pictures of the married couple together at various resorts or exotic and remote locations, but none with Benjamin present. It was sad, she thought, that the couple's lifestyle didn't appear to include their son but instead, seemed to revolve around *excluding* him.

Thinking she should try to warm up to the young ward she had been charged with looking after, Danica decided to see if she could convince Benjamin to join her downstairs for a night of television binge-watching. She made her way upstairs, hearing the sound of videogame gunshots and explosions getting louder as she approached the boy's bedroom door. Knocking twice, she called out to the boy.

"Benjamin, would you like to hang out with me downstairs and watch some tv? I'll let you choose."

"I'm playing my game," was his loud response. Then he continued, "And you don't have to worry about me all night. I'm just going to stay up here playing my game until I feel myself falling asleep. It'll be an easy paycheck for you."

Danica felt her shoulders drop at the boy's retort. She could hear the anguished pain in his voice but would respect his wishes with the optimistic hope that he would eventually change his mind.

"Ok, Benjamin," she shouted over the loud booming sounds erupting from his game console. "You know where I'll be if you need anything."

With that, Danica made her way back down the stairs and into the living room, where she couldn't help glancing at the large windows, once again, which now displayed her reflection as clearly as any mirror. The night had claimed the day, and with it, her view of the outside world.

She sat down on the comfortable leather couch, grabbed the remote from the glass coffee table, and powered on the tube, determined to do what she had hoped Benjamin would have joined her in doing: a night of unhealthy television binge-watching.

The screen lit up with the evening news. Danica would have strayed from the broadcast in favor of a police drama or a suspense thriller, but the display of "breaking news" flashing across the scrolling banner at the top of the newscast caught her attention. She decided to leave it for the time being.

"...the two inmates are reported to be armed and dangerous. Citizens are encouraged to contact the police if they witness either of the two men. Again, tonight's prison break has authorities baffled about how the two men, Roberto Hernandez and David Wehter, escaped incarceration from the Okten County Correctional Facility earlier this evening.

"Hernandez and Wehter were both serving consecutive life sentences for the rape and brutal slaying of three young women in Malmont Heights last April. The fugitives are suspected to be on their way back to their familiar surroundings before possibly attempting to flee the state. Authorities urge residents to stay indoors if possible and that travelers should avoid picking up hitchhikers.

"And now, a look at the weather. Amber?"

"Thank you, Chuck. Get ready for some high winds as the storm front begins to make its way in from the west of us..."

As if on cue, a sudden gust of wind slammed into the house, followed by the howling sound of its immense fury as it cascaded across the windows, startling Danica. As if hearing the upsetting news about the escaped convicts possibly heading back into the city wasn't bad enough, she had to deal with the frightening sound of the wind, too. Thankfully, she was currently in a nicer part of town where seedier characters were less likely to frequent. Still, the eerie thought lingered; what if..?

Reminding herself why she never watched the news, Danica flipped through the stations, looking for something a little less reality-based to settle on. Her thumb's continuous clicking eventually landed her on a B-grade vampire movie. It was a harmless enough flick but made all the more terrifying by the frightful sound of the howling wind outside the massive windows to her right.

Although she was blind to the outside, she could hear tree branches as they scraped against the tops of the windows just below the roofline, making her think of sharpened fingernails scraping across a chalkboard or the shrill sound made by a familiar, knife-gloved fiend as his razor-sharp blades traveled along a steel pipe, scaring children in their nightmares. Those thoughts were no good in helping to ease her mind. Perhaps getting herself a snack to enjoy while watching the movie, she thought, would help calm the wandering snapshots of frightening images swirling in her head.

Stepping into the large pantry, she heeded Alicia's words and grabbed herself a bag of *"food for poor people."* Placing the bag of popcorn into the microwave and setting the timer for two minutes, Danica leaned against the counter and stared at the kitchen window. She could see only blackness while the howling sound of the fierce wind continued as the storm loomed closer. Lost in her thoughts, she felt herself jump as the timer from the microwave dinged, signaling the popcorn was ready to be devoured. Pouring the bag's contents into a large bowl, she walked back into the living room to continue watching the awful movie she had started, when suddenly, a loud, banging noise from outside the window erupted, almost causing her to drop the bowl.

Danica's heart began to race as only the worst thoughts entered her mind. She placed the bowl of popcorn on the coffee table and slowly walked to the wall of windows. She could see the fear on her face from the reflection peering back at her. Swallowing the saliva that had formed in her mouth, she leaned forward and placed her forehead against the glass, hoping she'd be able to see something; anything. It was pointless. The night was so dark even the moon's light couldn't penetrate the threatening clouds above. She squinted to focus her eyesight but still, nothing. Then, three knocks suddenly pounded on the upper portion of the window, frightening Danica, and causing her to stumble back.

The three thuds she heard in rapid succession came from more than just a blown tree limb that had found its way against the exterior glass surface. Something or someone was out there. She could feel her muscles tense at the thought of who it might be as she recalled the evening's earlier newscast. For all she knew, there could be two crazed felons outside the house, staring in at her at that very moment with thoughts of raping her.

"Who's out there?" she shouted. "I'm not alone."

The wind howled its response along with what sounded like short, muffled coughing, or perhaps laughter. Danica realized her mind could be playing tricks on her, so she raced to the television remote and hit the mute button so she could concentrate on the peculiar sound from beyond the window. Again, a thud sound pierced the silence as she watched the image of herself vibrate in the windowpane.

"I'll call the police if you don't get out of here," she threatened loudly.

More wind ensued as the worst of the storm was impending. Danica felt herself trembling with nervous fear as she continued to stare at herself in the window, hoping it was only the force of the outside wind causing the strange, unnatural noises. She could open the sliding door leading to the back deck and peek out, but if there *was* someone out there, that could be inviting dire consequences. No, it was safer to remain behind locked doors.

With a thought, she quickly ran to the dining room and retrieved the business card from the sideboard, then made her way back into the living room, Alicia and Derek's voices echoing in her head.

"Do use the number sparingly, if at all possible," and *"What my wife is trying to express is, extreme emergencies only, please."*

Danica's fear from the sound of the wind could hardly be classified as an "extreme emergency," but she felt more comforted having the hotel's number at the ready, just in case. Just then, she thought of Benjamin, alone in his room, and her heart began to race faster. He probably had no idea there could be someone dangerous lurking outside the house. She debated whether or not she should bother him with what could turn out to be nonsense, her own insecurities. It was probably just the uneasiness of being in a stranger's home during a freak storm that had her on edge. Still, she thought, it wouldn't hurt to check on the boy.

She trudged up the stairs, her legs wobbly beneath her. She could still hear the sound of the boy's video game resounding through the hallway as she edged closer to his room, which made her feel better. As she reached for the doorknob, she heard his voice enter her head, his earlier words spoken harshly but with an air of sadness.

"And you don't have to worry about me all night. I'm just going to stay up here playing my game until I feel myself falling asleep. It'll be an easy paycheck for you."

Standing outside his door, Danica pulled her hand back, wondering what she would say to him. She wouldn't want to scare the boy or cause undue stress for something that could be nothing. The boy obviously wanted to be left alone, and until she could determine if there was an actual threat, she felt it would be best if she didn't thrust her unwarranted fears upon him. Logic and sensibility winning out, Danica turned and slowly trekked down the stairs, hoping with each step, the night would soon end.

When she arrived back in the living room, all seemed quiet and calm. The flickering lights from the muted tv were dancing on the wall behind the couch. The wind, which had been screaming like a gale force, had subsided as quickly as it had arrived. Danica stood motionless for a moment, listening intently for any further unusual sounds, but there were none. It would seem it was only the sound of the night wind that had caused her to panic. She felt relieved as she took in a deep breath and exhaled slowly, allowing her nerves to settle and calm.

With the worst of the fleeting storm seemingly past, Danica resumed her post on the couch. Pulling at the blanket that lay across the top of the couch, she covered her lap to get comfortable. She reached for the bowl of popcorn with one hand while the other snatched the television remote. She hit the mute button, once again, to return sound to the speakers but opted to switch the channel in favor of something considerably less thrilling. In minutes, she found herself halted on a classics sitcom station, enjoying a Honeymooners marathon. Finally, after the earlier scare she had been through, she was ready to earn that "easy paycheck."

"Danica. Danica, wake up," the voice said anxiously.

"Wh-what?" Danica responded, her eyes adjusting to the light. She had fallen asleep and found herself embarrassingly being awakened by Alicia. "I'm so sorry," Danica offered, "I must have drifted off. What time is it?"

"It's just past 2 a.m.," Alicia replied. "How'd everything go?"

"Oh, it was fine," Danica replied. "Yeah, just fine. You were right; Benjamin preferred to stay in his room."

"That's good," Alicia nodded. "Derek went upstairs to check on him."

Just then, Derek yelled from the second floor, "Where is he? He's gone!"

Danica felt her heart skip as she tossed the blanket aside and sprung to her feet. Derek came shuffling down the stairs like a mad man on a mission.

"He's not up there; he's not in his room!" Derek shouted excitedly. "I checked everywhere upstairs. He's not there."

"Well, he has to be here somewhere," Alicia returned as she scampered off toward the kitchen. "Benjamin, where are you?" she shouted, expecting to hear his response.

Derek glared at Danica, his face pale with fear. "Danica, you must know where he is. If you two are playing a game, it ends now. Where is my boy?"

"I... I don't know. It's not a game, I swear. Benjamin was in his room all night playing video games. He never even came downstairs."

"His game is still playing on his screen," Derek shouted, "but he's not there. When did you check on him last?"

"I... I..." Danica couldn't get the words out as she realized she *hadn't* checked on him. She had only made it as far as the door when she heard the exploding sound effects from his game and decided not to worry him about the strange sounds she had heard coming from the back...

Just then, Danica's eyes widened, and the blood rushed from her face.

"What is it, Danica?" Derek questioned, noticing the expression on her face.

Alicia sprinted back into the living room, "I can't find him anywhere, Derek." She then, too, noticed Danica's pale face as the babysitter turned her head toward the large windows.

"The noise," Danica mumbled. "Outside."

"The noise outside?" Derek questioned. "What are you mumbling about?" Even as the words exited his mouth, he was walking toward the slider door, puzzled by her comments. He opened the door and stepped out, and in the next moment, a blood-curdling scream disturbed the silence of the night air. Both Alicia and Danica ran to the door to bear witness to the horrifying sight of Benjamin's lifeless body hanging from the roof above, a knotted rope wrapped around the boy's neck and ankle.

It may have looked like an apparent suicide, but had Benjamin lived, he would have told a very different story. He was supposed to hang out with his friends that evening, and he wasn't going to let his punishment stand in his way. He had gathered the rope from the basement the day before and had climbed out his window onto the lower section of the roof to tie it to the heating exhaust pipe. It would stay coiled up there overnight. He knew his parents would be gone the next evening and would have a babysitter watching over him. He could outwit any babysitter. He would sneak out after his parents left and join up with his friends at the arcade. Then, he'd be back before they arrived home, and nobody would be the wiser.

Everything was going according to plan when he snuck out onto the roof that evening. With the rope in hand, who could have predicted a sudden forceful wind would cause Benjamin to lose his balance. As he lost his footing, he released the rope, which had then gotten tangled around his leg and neck as he struggled to prevent himself from sliding off the roof. As he plummeted, the rope pulled tautly around his neck. He managed to grab hold of the rope before the sudden jerk could snap his neck, but his airway was constricted, and he couldn't scream for help as his dangling body thrashed about violently, trying to gather oxygen. He kicked at the window a few times, trying to gain the babysitter's attention. He could see she was staring out at him, but she wasn't doing anything to help him. He expired after a couple of minutes, wondering what he had done that was so horrible that would keep her from wanting to save him. He wanted only to hang out with his friends. Instead, he found himself hanged.

Danica's guilt-ridden thoughts differed. She had allowed her fears to get the better of her. Had she not watched the evening news, perhaps she wouldn't have been as paralyzed by the sound of the night wind. Maybe she would have opened the slider to investigate the strange knocking she had heard. Maybe she could have saved Benjamin's life. The truth was, she may not have been able to save him at all. And now, as she stared in shock at the boy's dead body and watched as his parents struggled to remove him from his bindings, her thoughts drifted back on the evening. She recalled the father's stern grip on the boy's shoulder, the mother's callous, unfeeling words, the pictures that were noticeably absent of the boy's image, and she couldn't help but think that perhaps, Benjamin was now in a better place.

8

Lost and Found

It's been all over the news; they found another body in the woods. Stephanie Gardener, another girl from the university. That makes number five in as many months. There's probably more out there. That's why I'm heading there this morning. It was Julia's idea; she convinced me to go with her. She's on her way over now to pick me up.

It's scary to think about the girls that have gone missing from our campus. I didn't know any of them, thank God, but I'm sure I've seen them around. I've probably passed by them on my way to the Biology lab or sat near them in the campus food court. Were they in any of my classes? Had I given any of them a second glance? I never paid much attention to others, always so wrapped up in my studies. Well, I'm paying attention now.

The latest victim, Stephanie, was found by a couple of hikers whose afternoon must have been completely devastated by the terrible discovery. The news reported she had been missing for a couple of weeks. Like the other girls, her fingers had all been broken, and she had a large gash on the back of her head from having been struck with a blunt object, the cause of her death, according to the medical examiner. By the time Stephanie's body had been found, it had already shown signs of decay, and the bugs had found new nesting grounds in her mouth and nostrils. Not a pretty sight to imagine, let alone coming across it while you're supposed to be enjoying an early afternoon stroll through the woods.

It'll be different for us, though. Julia and I are heading out there for that exact purpose. It won't come as a complete shock if we happen upon a dead body. Not that I'm actually expecting to find anyone else; it's a vast expanse of forest, and the authorities have already combed much of it. But wouldn't that be something? I'd never been a part of anything like that before. Like the other couple, I would get interviewed and be on the news. It would be in all the papers too. I can see it now, *"Local girl finds another body, helps police with investigation."* I'd be a local celebrity. Ok, maybe I'm being a little overzealous. But even if none of that happens, it'll still be fun to hang out with Julia for the day; it's been a while since we've had the chance to chat, especially with our studies keeping us overly preoccupied. Speaking of which, that's probably her knocking now.

When I opened the door, I expected to find that Julia had taken this more seriously (it was her idea, after all), but instead, in typical fashion, there she was in her hiked-up "Pink" shorts with way too much of her legs exposed, flip-flop sandals, skin-tight crop top, and her silly, heart-shaped sunglasses. She looked like someone who was heading to the beach instead of someone who was about to go trudging through the woods.

"Hey, girl," Julia said in her best valley-girl impression. "You ready to get your groove on?"

"Oh my God, Julia, you're not exactly dressed for a hike."

"It's not a big deal," she said as she brushed by me into my dorm room, "I know a few easy trails."

"You *do* realize that we may have to wander off some trails to find what we're looking for?"

"Relax, Bev, you don't actually think we're going to find anyone out there, do you? I mean, Gross!"

"Well, if you didn't believe that, why did you suggest we go out there?"

"I don't know," Julia replied, a concerned look on her face, "it was something to do. I thought it would be fun. I didn't think you were going to take the whole thing about searching for bodies seriously. Wait, did you? Take it seriously, I mean?"

My heart sank when I heard that remark. I *had* taken it seriously. Someone is killing college girls and dumping their bodies in the woods. But apparently, Julia wasn't serious at all. That was disappointing, but I wasn't going to let it show. I put on a fake smile and closed the door.

"No, I knew you were just playing," I answered, holding my frustration in check. "I just wanted to see your reaction." It was a lie, but she didn't need to know that. Besides, we were still going for that hike, and it *had* been a while since we'd hung out like that. Once we're out there, though, I'll keep an eye out for anything out of the ordinary. I'm sure I can convince Julia to stick close to me if I stray from the trail.

"Oh my God!" Julia stated excitedly as she plopped herself into the loveseat and threw her legs up on the coffee table, one crossed over the other. "Did you hear about Professor Andrews?"

I shook my head, amazed at how easily she could change subjects. "No, what about him?"

"It's all over campus, Bev. You've got to get your head out of your books. Apparently, he was caught having sex in his office with Braden Stout."

"What? No way!" I suddenly was amazed at how easily *I* could get wrapped up in Julia's subject changes. "Braden's gay? But isn't he going out with Carrie Meyers?"

"Whatever," Julia responded. "Maybe he's bi. It doesn't matter. My point is, Beverly, he *was* going out with Carrie Meyers. Not anymore. She broke up with him after she'd found out what he'd been doing in his spare time. So, now he's available. What do you think;

should I try to hook up with him? I hear he's got a thing for blondes. I bet I could turn him straight."

I cringed. "Eewww! Julia. Apparently, he's got a thing for all sorts. Why would you want Professor Andrews' sloppy seconds?"

"I know, I know. But it's hard to think of Braden in that way. He is *so* hot. And you know I've had a crush on him since freshman year."

"Julia," I said sternly, slinging my backpack over my shoulder, "I *will not* let you degrade yourself by doing that. There are plenty of other guys out there."

She gave me a pouty face before I grabbed a water bottle from the counter and tossed it in her direction to distract her. "Now, let's go. We're losing daylight."

"Fine," Julia replied as she stood from the loveseat, squeezing the water bottle tight, "but I hope you can deal with the mental anguish I'm going through here."

I rolled my eyes, "Oh, brother. I'll do my best. Now, come on; let's get going."

Julia marched past me, a big smile on her face as she kissed into the air, "Mwah. Thanks, love."

I shook my head and felt a slight smirk come to my lips as I stepped out into the hall and closed the door behind us.

Julia was right; the trail she had chosen was an easy one. We'd already been on it for over half an hour before I realized there hadn't been a single obstacle in our way thus far. There hadn't even been a slight incline at all. It was pretty relaxing, being in such a secluded area of the forest, with nothing but the sound of the birds and the subtle breeze rustling through the leaves, guiding us onward. I was surprised, however, to see there weren't many others out here enjoying the beautiful weather. We had only passed by one other person shortly after we entered the trail, and from the looks of his sweat-soaked shirt, he had probably been out here jogging since the butt crack of dawn.

I kept my head up, scanning from side to side, looking for anything unusual: a break in the trail, drag marks in the dirt, signs of a struggle. There was nothing. As trails went, this probably wasn't one a killer would have found himself upon, but still, I continued to focus while making small talk.

"So, what's gonna happen to him, anyway?" I asked.

"With who?" Julia replied, keeping her eyes to the ground.

"Professor Andrews. You know, with the whole sex scandal thing."

"They've already suspended him," she answered, "pending the outcome of their investigation. It's a done deal, though. He's not coming back. He'll probably collect a nice severance and be on his way to another college in another state somewhere."

"It's not surprising; it happens all the time."

"Yeah, to the three P's:" Julia continued, "Priests, Professors, and Producers."

"You forgot Pig executives," I added.

"Ok, four P's."

We both laughed for a minute until something caught my eye on the side of the trail.

"Hey, what's that?" I pointed ahead of me and to the left. Julia lifted her shades and squinted to get a clearer view of what it was to which I was directing her attention. She never was very focused.

"What?" she asked. "What is it I'm supposed to be looking at?"

"You don't see it?" I quickly shuffled ahead of her to grab the item from the ground. It was a large rock, slightly bigger than my hand. Heavy too. The side against my palm was rounded and smooth, but the other side was jagged and sharp and covered in what appeared to be dried blood.

"Look at this; I think that's blood."

"Shut up! No way," Julia stated, shocked at the idea of it.

"I'm telling you, it's blood. You've seen the news. The police said each of the victims was struck in the back of the head with a blunt object. What if this is what the killer used?"

"Let me see it," Julia requested, holding out her hand.

I could see I piqued her curiosity as I handed her the rock. She slid her sunglasses up onto the top of her perfectly combed blonde hair and began inspecting the red-stained stone more intently.

"Nah, I don't think that's blood," she argued. "It looks more like someone painted it."

"Painted a rock? Out here? And then they just threw it to the side of the trail? Are you serious?" My voice might've been sounding like I was a bit annoyed. A nervous look came upon Julia.

"I don't know," she answered. "It's just kind of creepy to think that it could be blood."

"But I bet it *is* blood," I continued while making my way over to where I first found the rock. "And look at this," I said, circling my hands in the air above the immediate area. "Tell me this doesn't look like something bad had happened here."

I was surprised, myself. The ground on both sides of the trail was blanketed with leaves, creating a level carpet of browns and yellows that, for the most part, looked undisturbed. But where the blood-covered rock was situated, bunches of leaves were spread apart and rustled aside, forming what looked like a secondary path through the woods. It almost looked like something (or someone) had been dragged from the trail.

"I don't like this," Julia stated. "You're getting a little too excited."

"But don't you see, Julia? There could be another body out there."

"Or it could be a bear or something," Julia protested. "You don't know."

"That's just it, though," I responded. "We *don't* know. But if there *is* someone out there, maybe even still alive, shouldn't we try to find them?"

Julia shrugged her shoulders and shook her head.

"I'm going out there to check it out," I told her. "You coming with me?"

"No, Bev," she replied, "don't go out there."

"I'm sorry, Julia; I have to. Someone could need help."

I started off the trail, following the disheveled path of leaves. "Just stay there," I yelled back. "I won't be long."

"Beverly," Julia cried, "don't leave me here."

"You're welcome to come with me," I yelled from a distance. I could hear Julia's pleas fade out as I followed the broken path of leaves down an embankment. I hated leaving her like that, but she clearly didn't want to come along, and I couldn't stand idly by, knowing there could be someone lying in the middle of the woods, fighting for their life. Am I crazy? Maybe. For all I know, Julia could be right about this being the tracks of a bear who had been rummaging for food. But what if I'm right? What if the killer had dragged someone off the path? Maybe the killer was the jogger we passed earlier? Or worse, what if the killer was still at the scene where he dragged his victim? I was starting to spook myself. I could see the path I was following continued for quite a distance. I realized then that it probably wasn't the smartest idea to be following it alone. I decided to stop where I was and head back.

I thought I'd hear Julia still yelling for me once I made it back up the hill. When I didn't, I figured she must have finally given up, realizing I was too stubborn to listen to her, but when I made it back to the walking trail, she was nowhere in sight. What *was* in sight, however, were two drag marks dug into the soil, like feet scraping along the ground, leading to the opposite side of the road. My stomach flopped, and my heart began to pound in my chest. I glanced at my watch to note the time. I had only been away for less than ten minutes. Wherever she was, it couldn't be far from here.

"Julia!" I yelled, hoping for a response. "Julia, where are you?"

I received no reply, which made me that much more nervous. I followed the two drawn tracks in the dirt over to the other side of the trail; that was when I saw what made my hands begin to tremble. It was one of Julia's pink and turquoise sandals, flipped upside down in a pile of leaves. My mind started racing as I called out to her again.

"Julia! Can you hear me?"

Again, nothing.

"Julia, if this is a joke, I'm going to be so mad at you."

Only the sound of silence returned. I began to mumble to myself.

"Come on, Julia; come on. Please don't let this be happening right now. All right, Beverly, get yourself together. You just went out in search of a total stranger; you can certainly go in search of a friend. You can do this."

I hesitantly stepped off the trail in the direction of the drag marks. This wasn't just a fantasy any longer; the hopeful wishes of gaining recognition by finding a girl's body, of stepping into the spotlight and gaining my fifteen minutes of fame; this was real.

The path of disturbed leaves on this side was much narrower. It stood to reason. Julia was pretty thin. The victim dragged from the other side (I'm sticking to the idea that there was another victim at some point) must have been a bit larger.

"What are you doing, Beverly?" I continued to mumble, hoping to distract myself from my fear. "You're already condemning your friend. She's just lost, that's all. You'll see. She's probably sitting against a tree somewhere, rubbing the ankle she twisted because she insisted on wearing those ridiculous flip-flops on a hiking trip."

I followed the rustled path deeper into the woods, hoping it would be just as easy on the way out. The last thing I needed was to get lost after finally finding Julia. Where the hell was she? Why did I leave her alone?

I called out again, "Julia!" with the same result. I quickened my pace as the wind picked up, swirling the loosened leaves behind me in all directions. If I didn't find her soon, would there even be a path left to follow? Panic started to set in as I heard the upper branches of the trees crashing and scraping against one another, making awful creaking sounds. I stopped and spun in place, looking all around the dense forest. I saw only trees and leaves, continuing in all directions. It was disorienting.

"Julia, please! Call back to me."

Nothing. Nothing but the distorted path of rustled leaves before me, leading me further into the unknown. I continued onward, calling for Julia and begging for her to answer. The answer never came. I looked at my watch again and was shocked. Before I realized it, I had been searching for Julia for almost forty minutes.

All I could think about was how this day was supposed to be so different. I didn't want to be out here alone like this. I've been following this path, hoping my friend would turn up. She's probably back at the trail, wondering where I am, having only just stepped into the woods to go pee behind a tree right before I showed up. That's probably it. But why wouldn't she have called back to me? Was she too embarrassed to let someone like me know that someone like her could drop trow in the middle of the woods to do their business? It *would* be just like her to worry about something like that.

I was just about to give up on the search and turn back when I spotted a glimpse of color ahead of me by a large oak. Curious, yet scared of what I suspected it to be, I cautiously strode to the tree, where at the base, half-buried in the leaves, was Julia's other sandal. I felt the color leave my face as I suddenly felt light-headed. I now knew with certainty that she was out here somewhere. Only, I had no idea where.

I bent down to pick up the sandal, and when I rose, I heard a twig snap behind me. Before I could react, I felt the blow to the back of my head. The ground rushed up to greet me, the leaves doing their best to break my fall. I might have blacked out for a moment, but hitting the ground jolted me back to consciousness. Not that being awake did me any good. I was completely out of it, weak, dizzy, only barely feeling my body as it was forcefully rolled over to face upward. My vision was blurred, and my thoughts were erratic and unfocused. I slid my hand across the ground, reaching for the tree, but it never made it. Instead, I felt the cold hand of the person who did this to me as they wrenched on my index finger, snapping it backward. I tried to scream, but it came out as a faint gurgling sound as blood spat out from my lips and dribbled down my cheek. Then the sound of my middle finger cracking filled the otherwise silent air.

By the time my fourth finger had been broken, all pain had left my body. I could feel myself fading, slipping away. A calmness came over me when I realized this was it. But there was also a sense of sadness; this was what the other girls had gone through; this was what Julia had to endure. I couldn't save her. Why did I have to go off and leave her alone? All because I wanted so badly to be recognized. How ridiculous. And now, even with my thoughts quickly deserting me, I realized I *would* get that recognition after all, but for the worst of reasons. I *would* be on the news, and I *would* have a headline in the papers: *"Another local girl's body discovered in the woods."* It's not exactly as I had envisioned.

And just as eternal darkness was about to claim its next soul, a moment of clarity swept over me. My vision cleared enough for me to catch a glimmer of my assailant standing over me, with her long blonde hair and hiked-up "Pink" shorts, a wicked smile on her face. It was…

Three weeks later.

It's been all over the news; they found another body in the woods. Beverly Greene, another girl from the university. That makes number six in as many months. There's probably more out there. That's why I'm heading to those woods this morning with my new friend, Julia. It was her idea; she convinced me to go with her. She's on her way over now to pick me up.

9

Paint the Town Red

We had been warned. That's what the red "X"s were all about. If you arrived at your establishment to find one painted across your door, you'd better close up shop and get the hell out of town before the enforcers showed up to collect; because they wouldn't be after the money this time.

Extortion was big business - bigger than any of our small mom-and-pop shops. And if you wanted to stay open, you had to pay. The price was high, probably higher than it should have been for such a small backwater town as ours, but if you didn't pay, they extracted an even heavier toll; one there was no coming back from.

It had been a few years since the three men first showed up, offering their "protection" services in exchange for "fair" compensation as if they worked for the mafia of old. The thing is, "fair" must have been defined differently in the dictionaries they used, because it certainly felt like we were being squeezed out of our very livelihoods.

The sheriff and his crew were no help. They quickly learned to look the other way as soon as the envelopes of cash started showing up. They were getting richer while the rest of us were getting poorer. Every month, like clockwork, they'd get paid, and all they had to do for it was turn the other way and pretend like nothing was happening. It was sickening.

The game was easy, the rules even easier; if you owned a business, you'd forfeit two thousand dollars of your monthly earnings. For the first year, the three well-dressed heavies came calling each month to collect in person, barging into our stores and demanding the money be paid, or there would be unfavorable consequences. It was all new to us, so after a few business owners refused to pay that first month, the goon squad gave them a second chance, deciding only to break a few of their fingers. It could have been much worse, as we later discovered after Tom Bensen couldn't take their demands anymore. After about the sixth or seventh month, he had let a month slide without payment, explaining he could barely keep his store afloat and hardly survive on what they let him keep. He had already had the fingers on his left hand broken months earlier from being one of the obstinate owners who refused to pay the first month. That second time, however, surprisingly, they left him alone. Or so we thought.

The next morning, Tom arrived at his store to find a big red X painted from the top corners of his door down to the bottom corners like police tape cordoning off a crime scene. One would have thought it was the local riff-raff graffitiing storefronts, except by the next day, it was *actual* police tape canvassing the door.

Tom's body was found beaten and bloody behind one of his display cabinets, the side of his head caved in, with the murder weapon, the granite base of a trophy from the local little league club he had sponsored, lying on the floor beside him. Mrs. Pesiak was the first customer of the day that morning. The poor woman had walked right in, the door still unlocked from the night before. Whoever it was that had killed Tom wanted his body to be found easily. It was a message left for the rest of us. Pay with money, or pay with your life.

We all knew who it was, even the authorities, but there was no evidence to link anyone to the crime. Tom's murder would go unresolved, though it gathered a lot of media coverage those first few weeks, too much so for the thugs to take a liking to it. They couldn't afford another public incident alerting the Feds. Something like that would disrupt their operation. So, a few months later, when Bruce Thouin's shop door had the familiar red X painted on it, his body *wasn't* found dead. It just wasn't found. At all.

It was a shame. I had just had a conversation with Bruce two weeks earlier about paying the money. He was telling me how he wasn't going to do it, and I urged him to reconsider, especially after what had happened to Tom. When I saw the red X on his door, I knew he hadn't listened. And then, he was gone, vanished without a trace. That's when it sunk in for most of us; the painted red X was an epitaph of sorts; the last thing you'd see before the end.

I was fortunate enough to be in the good graces of the extortionists, having kept up with my payments from the start. I didn't want any trouble, and my business was doing well, especially after I absorbed much of Tom's inventory after his death. He didn't have any family, so everything was auctioned off. I had a little money saved, so I bought most of it to bolster my own sales. And why not? Tom had a decent business, dealing in antiquities. He just lacked good business sense. Once I took it over, my profits almost doubled. And *my* increase meant an increase for the mob wannabes, who insisted I up my payment to four thousand dollars to cover their recent loss, which I graciously did without an argument. They liked that. It's how I was eventually able to convince them of the lockboxes.

Every month during that first year, the three of them would shakedown store proprietors during working hours, scaring customers with their threats while stealing from us. When they came for my payment, which I always had at the ready, I asked if I could make a small suggestion that would benefit everyone. In the most non-confrontational way I could, I advised them that their unwelcome and aggressive presence each month, showing up during working hours, was scaring away customers, thereby making it difficult for some owners to meet their demands. I suggested lockboxes be installed on each storefront for the owners to drop their payments into. Then, the money could be easily collected after-hours, with no interruption to daily business and no heavy-handed threats required. Customers would feel safer and be more willing to shop if they no longer needed to worry that their shopping experience could be suddenly interrupted by the uncomfortable monthly intrusion. It was sound advice. They weren't the brightest lot, but they were smart enough to know I was right.

I convinced the other store owners that this was the best and easiest way to ensure everyone's safety. It also gave customers peace of mind. So, the following month, lockboxes, to which the three goons had the only keys, were installed on the doors of every business. We were all instructed to have our full payment dropped into the boxes by the first of every month, or the punishment would be steep. Each of their crew would then take turns collecting the money each month during the wee hours of the night. Everything seemed to be going smoothly until after the third month when the last of the trio supposedly went rogue, and on his night to collect, he stole the money and fled. The next day, the remaining two paid us all a visit, threatening to remove the lockboxes since the idea had cost them one of their men. I managed to talk them down, but they demanded we all cough up an additional thousand dollars for the next month to make up for their loss.

The additional money wasn't an issue for me; I had since started selling merchandise that Bruce had been selling in his shop before his disappearance. It only made sense. After he was gone, there was a void to fill, and people had relied on his products for years. I had enough capital, so I got into the small electronics business, picking up where he had left off.

Although I could afford the extra thousand the goons had demanded, it wasn't as easy for others, as was discovered when Sam Forester's front door was defaced with a splattering of red paint in the shape of an X. We all knew what was going to happen next, but I couldn't stand by without at least trying to stop it.

I marched into the police station to have words with the sheriff, but it was clear he was a slave to the money being provided to him and his staff for letting the criminals continue their felonious enterprise. He said if I could prove who graffitied the establishment, he could slap a misdemeanor charge on the miscreant, but other than that, no other crime had been committed. As I said, extortion was big business. I left the station fuming and with a heavy heart, wondering what would happen to Sam. We never found out, as he went missing the next day. I suppose he could have run, fearing for his life, but that's just wishful thinking on my part.

I miss Sam; he was a good guy. But he should have paid, dammit, even if he had to draw from whatever little savings he had. He could have made it up in a few months. Instead, he was gone, most likely dead in a ditch somewhere.

The man had been a cornerstone in this town. But with him gone, I felt I owed it to him and the community to keep his auto parts store open. I had enough cash flow coming in from the electronics business to buy the store from his family. His wife never wanted any part in the business anyway, and I figured they could use the money. It was just good business sense.

After a few more months of no missteps, another red X was obtrusively displayed on Ruth Tanner's door. She had always been a sweet woman, and with such a lovely craft store. But then, she too was gone, vanishing into the night. It could have been avoided had she just paid. Why didn't she pay?

I think back over the past three years since the outsiders first showed up, and I realize I've been pretty lucky compared to some. Things could have turned out a lot differently for me had I been stubborn about paying way back in the beginning. Most people now have come to terms with paying their dues; it's just the cost of doing business. And yes, I did say *most* people.

It's the start of a new month, and just yesterday, another shop owner hadn't paid. The other price they will instead end up paying weighs heavily on my mind. When are these people going to learn? The situation hasn't changed; there's still a heavy cost. I shake my head in disgust as I make my way down the wooden staircase to my dark basement. I can hear the muted grumblings of the three criminals who had plagued our small town for over a year, the cloths stuffed tightly in their mouths and held in place by the layers of duct tape wrapped around their heads. They would have continued their terrorizing ways had I not done something about it. The first one was easy pickings once I learned their schedule. It helped that he was making his collection rounds alone. After him, it became more difficult since the other two decided to collect the dues together, neither one of them having enough trust in the other to go it alone. It took me a few months to figure it out, but I did it; I got them both. You should have seen their faces when they woke up and saw their former partner, who they'd thought had run away with the cash, tied up like a helpless fish in a net. They were in the same unfortunate circumstance, each of them bound to a separate lally column.

Their bodies have withered a bit since I first took them hostage, not from lack of sustenance (I've fed them quite well), but from what they have forced me to extract from them. If the other shopkeepers don't fall in line, these three won't be around much longer.

Making my way over to them, I grab the blade from atop my workbench, and the pail from beneath it. Their bound bodies begin to squirm in fear. They know what's coming; they've felt the sting before. A cut here, a slice there, my pail will soon have a fair amount of the crimson liquid flowing from their wounds, enough to send a much-needed message.

I mentioned it before, extortion is big business. But only if people pay. And last night, Hirochi Kenzie did not. He'll have a red X on his door come morning, painted with the blood of those who set me on this path. After all, someone had to take over for them, so why not me? It's just good business sense. The police still get their cash, businesses still deposit into the lockboxes, and nobody's the wiser, all of them thinking it's these three lowlives who are responsible.

Eventually, I'm confident everyone will have enough sense to make their payments on time. And I'll do my part to make sure of it, even if I have to paint this whole damn town red.

10

A Score to Settle

The doorbell caught Jeremy's attention as he descended the ladder. He was expecting his visitor, which is why he had already been making his way down from the attic. He had been there most of the morning, sifting through the boxes left behind, boxes filled with items from a bygone era. His parents didn't leave him much, only the house and the cherished memories made within; those and the packed boxes of mostly useless treasures stored in the darkened space above the ceiling. He was accepting of that. But he had found something of interest, which was the reason for his guest's invitation, as he opened his front door.

"Hey, Steve," Jeremy greeted. "Thanks for coming over."

"Yeah, of course," Steve replied. "It sounded urgent. What's the emergency?"

"Oh, no emergency. Sorry if I sounded excited. I was going through some boxes my parents had in the attic, and well, I know how you're a history buff and all. I found something I thought you might be interested in checking out."

"Yeah, sure," Steve responded. "I'm always up for learning about the past. Whatever you've got, maybe it'll be worth some money for you."

"Oh, I'm not interested in the money. But I would like to get your thoughts on this particular item."

"Sure thing. Whatcha got?"

"I left it up in the attic. Follow me." Jeremy waved his hand forward, leading the way to the lowered ceiling ladder.

"I still can't believe your parents are gone," Steve stated in a somber tone as he followed his friend down the hallway.

"It's ok; it wasn't unexpected. They had both been sick for quite some time. I'm just glad it's finally over. They don't have to worry about the pain anymore."

"I hear you there."

Jeremy climbed the narrow, wooden ladder first, followed by his curious friend. The light from a dimly-lit bulb barely pierced the blackness as they entered the small rectangular entryway. Ahead of them, as the attic opened up into a larger space, a brighter light from a standing lamp cut through the floating particles of dust.

On the floor beneath it were open boxes, their contents scattered about in organized piles. Jeremy led the way into the brighter space, pointing at a small wooden chest beside a dilapidated chair.

"It's just over here," he said. "Have a seat." He pointed to the rickety-looking chair with peeled-off paint chips that decorated the floor beneath it. Steve hesitated, showing concern. "Don't worry; it'll support you. It's been supporting *my* fat ass all morning."

Steve nodded but slowly slid into the seat anyway, hoping it wouldn't collapse. Jeremy opened the wooden chest, pulled out a dusty book, and placed it on his friend's lap.

"Is this it?" Steve asked. "Is this what you wanted me to look at?"

"It is," Jeremy replied. "It's a journal that belonged to my Great Grandfather. Open it up; check it out."

It was a heavy book, about the size of a ream of paper. Steve swiped his hand across the soft cover, removing a swath of dust from the worn, black surface. Its edges were torn, and there was a smattering of small tears along its spine, which was bound together with frayed twine. Steve carefully opened the worn cover, fearful it might fall apart in his hands. The paper within was yellow with age, and discolored stains marked many of the pages, probably tarnished by drops of saliva-drenched chewing tobacco that dripped from the writer's mouth while he transcribed his thoughts on paper. On the opening page, written in faded black ink, were the words *"Property of Jeremiah Litchfield."*

"Jeremiah, huh?" Steve inquired without asking an actual question.

"Yes," Jeremy nodded, responding to his curious friend, "I was named after my Great Grandfather."

"Look at that," Steve added, "I learned something new."

"Keep reading," Jeremy nudged. "I think you'll find it interesting."

Steve turned the page and read the first entry, dated August 17th, 1885. It was a personal account of Jeremiah's feelings about the then recently elected Grover Cleveland to the Presidency of the United States. He then paused in his reading to remark about it.

"This is amazing," he said. "Have you read it? I mean, the whole thing?"

"Yeah," Jeremy replied. "Well, I've read most of it, anyhow."

Steve flipped through a few pages, landing on an entry dated November 9th, 1889.

New fella came into town today. Didn't like his looks. He was gussied up proper like he was the Governor. He turned his nose up at most folks he walked by, but I would have nothing doing with that. I marched over to him and confronted him about his uppity behavior. I guess I was in a mood and rarin' to start me a fight.

'Turns out he's a big shot lawyer lookin' to relocate from New York City. We struck up a friendly con-

versation before he invited me to sip down some whiskey at the saloon. I couldn't refuse. Besides, being all friendly with a lawyer could work out in my favor someday.

Steve peeled back another small bunch of pages, skipping past a handful of years, settling on a page with a large tear in it that had since been repaired with scotch tape.

February 20th, 1892
    That woman was a sight to behold. She had such a pretty smile; it just about set my heart tumblin' when she looked my way. Her name's Lucille, I learned. I wouldn't rightly think she'd be interested in a man of my paltry means, but if she were, I'd make her mine, for sure. I'd treat her good too, like a woman like that ought to be treated. I heard her talking with Mrs. Peabody at the Mercantile. She's not beholden or committed to a man. Maybe I do stand a chance with her, after all. I just gotta get up the nerve to do something other than stare from a distance.

Steve skimmed more of the page before tilting his head sideways to glance at the remaining thickness.
    "This is quite a bit of writing your Great Grandfather did. Is it like this through the whole thing?"
    "Pretty much," Jeremy replied. "Most of it is plain everyday stuff for the times, you know, saloon fights,

outhouses, and washing clothes by the river. Oh, and there's a page or two where he talks about having to put down his horse."

"Ok," Steve said while shrugging his shoulders, "but these are personal accounts of your Great Grandfather's life. Don't get me wrong; I think it's cool, but this is *your* family history. What am I supposed to get out of this; why did you need *me* here?"

"Well, I dog-eared some of the pages," Jeremy replied. "I thought you'd be interested in some of it. As I said, most of it is him ranting about meaningless things, but there's also something interesting that happened that I wanted to get your take on. I think you'll notice where I started folding…yeah, there it is; about halfway into the book."

"Yeah, I've got it," responded Steve. "Let's see what we have here." He opened to the first marked page.

April 16th, 1899

I just learned Lucille's gonna have our child. I don't think there's a happier man in this town.

Steve looked up from his reading, "Oh, hey, your Great Grandfather got his girl."

"He did," Jeremy said with a smirk. "Keep reading; the interesting stuff is coming up soon."

I'm gonna tell her about the parcel of land I bought for us. It's on the outskirts of town. She's gonna fall in love with it. She deserves every bit of happiness for what she's given me.

Steve finished the passage and flipped to the next folded corner in the book.

January 10th, 1900

We made it to the new century, and we brought with us a baby boy. Little Jessup was born this morning, and he already has more hair than his old man and a smile that would make the ladies swoon. Lucille's gonna raise our son right, teach him better than I ever learned, but I'll teach him everything he needs to know to be a man. He'll never be wanting for nothin'.

Flipping even more pages, Steve had so far enjoyed what he was reading until he came upon the next saved entry.

August 4th, 1910

He killed her; I know it was him. She meant everything to me, and he took her from us. No child should have to grow up without his mama. That rat bastard had pretended to be my friend for nearly twenty years, even helping Jessup with his school work on occasion when he'd come out this way to visit. I couldn't believe the man's audacity when he called in the Sheriff's deputies, accusing me of killing Lucille. I was the one asking for his help, and he had me arrested. I found his handkerchief, his favorite one, lying beside her body. It's how I know he's the one that did that to her. He raped and killed my sweet Lucile, but they didn't believe me. He thinks because he's this big-shot lawyer, he can have me put away for life when I didn't do anything. They can lock me up, but nothing's gonna stop me from getting at him, even if it kills me. I'll never rest until this is over.

"Holy shit!" Steve exclaimed. "Is this for real? Was your Great Grandmother killed?"

"I never heard about it before," Jeremy replied, "but I'm thinking it's all real. Especially after I read more." He pointed to the book again, urging Steve to continue. Steve pulled aside a bunch of pages leading to the next folded corner.

September 30th, 1939

Dad's gone. He rotted away in that cell just like they wanted him to. They gave me his belongings, which weren't much at all: a pocket knife, twenty-three cents, a half-smoked pack of cigarettes, which he'd taken up several years after his incarceration, and this journal. I've read the entire thing twice. I figured the least I could do was continue what he started.

I never knew what he knew about the day Mom died until I read about it. I remember the man he talked about, the one with the handkerchief. He always seemed so nice, but now I know the truth. I promise you this, Dad; one way or another, that man will pay for Mom's death.

"Wow," Steve said. "That was Jeremiah's son writing that: your Grandfather. Did he get the man responsible?"

"I don't think so," Jeremy replied. "I mean, I never met my Grandfather, he died before I was born, but based on later entries in the journal...well, you'll see what I mean."

Steve skipped over another handful of pages to get to the next marked section.

March 24th, 1982
And so, here I am, continuing what my father and his father did before, keeping track of my progress in this old journal. The one difference is I've managed to do what neither of them could; I've tracked what's left of the man's family here. My dad made a promise to his father, and he made me promise the same. The man responsible for raping and killing my Grandmother is long dead, but the score hasn't been settled yet. If I can't kill the man responsible, I'll take his grandson.

"Dude, that's your dad talking all crazy."

"Tell me about it," Jeremy responded. "This is all kinda freaking me out. I never knew any of this. And it's not done yet. There's more."

"Are you sure you want me reading about some of this stuff? I mean, it seems like it should remain private."

"It's fine; it's all in the past now. I'm telling you, it gets even more interesting. Listen, I'm gonna go get myself a beer. Do you want one?"

"Uh, yeah, sure," Steve replied. "As long as it's not that Lite stuff I catch you drinking now and again."

"No problem; I'll be right back."

As his friend descended the ladder, Steve turned back to the book, opening to the next dog-eared page.

July 5th, 1982

I'm sorry Dad, Grandpa; I tried. I couldn't do it. I had it all planned out. I was going to kill him last night during the fireworks celebration in town. The spectacle, the loud explosions, nobody would've seen or heard a thing. I was ready to finally exact my revenge, our revenge, on the killer's ancestor, but he had his boy with him. His son was about the same age as my boy. Once I saw him, I thought of my little Jeremy and what he would go through if he were to lose me. After that, I couldn't take from the boy his father. I know I've let you down. Please forgive me.

Steve saw there was one final folded page near the end of the journal and jumped right to it. There was a single entry on the page, along with an old Polaroid picture tucked into the seam. Steve pulled the photo out and looked at it, squinting his eyes as he tilted his head in thought at what he was looking at. There were four people in the photo: two adults and two children. It was vaguely familiar to him, as he recalled that particular fourth of July celebration with his dad, the way he was smiling and holding the sparkler so proudly. He had met a new friend that day, the other boy in the picture: Jeremy. He then glanced down at the page to read what had been written. It was a single line of text under what was today's date that read:

Rest easy now, Great Grandpa.

Steve heard the creaking of the floorboards behind him just as the hammer smashed into the back of his head.

11

Screams in the Dark

Every night, it was the same thing. She couldn't escape it. The screams always came when she closed her eyes. All Rebecca wanted was to sleep. It used to be so easy for her. She'd close her eyes and drift off into her make-believe world of fantasies until the morning light cast away the sleeping hours. But that was before the screams started, and her nights were no longer hers to control. That was her reality.

For the better part of two months, Rebecca had been losing sleep because of the awful screeching noise. She had become irritable, angry, and unable to concentrate during the day. She had tried medicating herself with over-the-counter sleep aids, but the horrible screams had more sway over her nights than the effects of the drugs. She had even thought about speaking with a sleep therapist, thinking the doctor might have been able to offer some explanation as to why she was hearing the unpleasant shrieks, but she never went, and the screams persisted.

They had started as subtle moans, waking her from her slumber as she stayed curled up beneath the blankets, listening intently for any movement. There were no footsteps, no sounds of anything in her apartment being moved or taken by an intruder, just the moans that would eventually fade, swallowed by the night, finally allowing her to succumb to the darkened silence. As the evenings rolled on, however, the moans became louder, lasted longer, and were harder to ignore, even if she were able.

After only a few short nights, the hushed moans, which she later wished had remained, were replaced with the harsh screaming she had been forced to endure night after sleepless night.

She remembered the first time she was woken by the abrasive racket. She jumped out of bed from the startling noise which seemed to be echoing off every wall in her bedroom. Her heart racing, she ran from the room in search of a dying cat, or perhaps, one in heat crying out for a mate. The noise came at her from all directions; it was everywhere, bombarding her senses. It was so loud and pervasive, causing her to cringe as her eyes squinted and her jaw tightened. Then, as if she had somehow willed it, it ceased. She was eventually able to fall back to sleep, unable to discern what it was that had disturbed the night. But that was only the first time the unsettling screams haunted the darkness.

They came every night after that, almost as soon as her eyelids closed, ringing in her ears like a severe case of tinnitus that she couldn't shake. She would have gladly welcomed that bitter annoyance over what sounded like the cries of a tortured soul being burned alive in the depths of Hell.

Early on, she'd had some theories, noticing the screams would only erupt when it was time for bed. So, she'd stay awake, staring at the ceiling in complete silence, except for the sound of the wall clock's second-hand as it ticked away the minutes, reminding her that the morning was fast approaching. When she *did* manage to fall asleep, it was as she suspected; the screams lashed out with such vengeance, invading her skull.

Most nights, she'd lie awake in bed, squeezing her eyes shut as tightly as she could and pressing her palms to her ears, hoping to minimize the intolerable noise. It never worked. Hour after hour, the screams became deafening until her alarm would sound, signaling the end of her restless night, but with it, the start of her comatose morning.

After weeks of sleep deprivation, Rebecca had thought of a way of putting an end to the agonizing torment. How easy it would have been to remove herself from this life, finally silencing the relentless screams. But as she sat in the tub and brought the cold steel of the sharp razor to her wrist, at that moment, she couldn't help but notice the sweet sound of calming silence. She had forgotten what it felt like to be overwhelmed by its healing effects. She had once had nights like that, and in that most vulnerable of moments, she had concluded, she was determined to have nights like that again. The razor found its way into the trash bin by the toilet.

Unfortunately, the screams in the dark didn't end as soon as the self-harming thoughts did. They continued to batter Rebecca's evenings the moment she'd allow her heavy eyes to close. She knew of their harmful routine, the way the screams toyed with her. If she was awake, silence won out. If she tried to sleep, the awful screeching began. Although she hadn't had more than a full night's sleep in two months, she supposed that the lack of sleep was better than hearing the loud shrieks that pummeled her brain.

The sleeping pills and her intermittent dozing hadn't been enough to solve the problem, so she decided to take the opposite approach; overdosing on cups of coffee to try and stay awake. For days, Rebecca slogged around the apartment like a zombie, her self-induced insomnia taking a toll on her mental and physical state. She would find herself standing in front of her apartment window, staring out across the parking lot for hours, never remembering even walking to the window at all. She would binge-watch television shows throughout the night, having no idea what any of them were about, only cognizant of the flashes of light and color splashing across the screen. Her speech was becoming slow and unintelligible. Her brain was urging her to get some sleep, but she wouldn't listen to its sound advice. She couldn't. She knew if she tried to sleep, the unbearable screams would return, and that would be worse than anything else she could imagine.

But the screams *did* return, and in the worst way imaginable. Rebecca had been sitting at the kitchen table, drinking her umpteenth cup of high-octane liquid caffeine, when suddenly, the wretched screams exploded, tearing the quiet morning asunder. It was seven-thirty in the morning, the sun had already penetrated through the window coverings, and more perplexing, she was awake. The screams that had previously only haunted her sleep had suddenly found a way to devastate her life while she was awake.

Rebecca squeezed her hands to her ears, unable to withstand the screeching sound. As hard as she tried, they wouldn't go away. She stood from the table and began to pace wildly from the kitchen to the living room and back, grabbing and pulling at her hair to try and distract herself from the terrible screams that filled the apartment. Nothing she did seemed to work; the screams were too piercing to ignore.

Without another thought, or at least without a rational one, she ran to the bookshelf and grabbed the thickest, heaviest hardcover she could find. It wasn't what she had planned, but she needed to make the screaming stop; it was destroying her life. Holding the book with both hands, she swung it up, smashing it into her forehead as hard as she could, thinking it would end the earsplitting noise, but the screams persisted. Again and again, the cover of the book slammed hard into Rebecca's head but still offered no relief from the violating screams. Everything started becoming a blur as the incessant cries assaulted her ears from every direction, just as the book similarly assaulted her forehead. She felt a rage boiling from within as she clutched the book ever tighter in her hands, squeezing it with every ounce of her being. Then, in the next instant, darkness overwhelmed her, and the screams suddenly ceased.

Opening her eyes, she found herself lying on the living room floor, the bloodstained book beside her outstretched arm. The apartment was silent; the screams had faded into oblivion. She lay still, glaring across the unswept floor, enjoying the serene moment that had escaped her for too long, and she smiled. When the moment had passed, she slowly sat up on her knees and glanced at the book that had fallen from her hands when she passed out and hit the floor. The cover was creased, and the spine was beyond repair. Smeared blotches of dried blood decorated its hard shell, making the title unreadable. Droplets of blood had spattered across the wood floor, bouncing from the book's cover upon impact. She imagined her forehead was more damaged than the book, yet she didn't feel any pain other than a mild headache coming along. Carefully rubbing her bloody fingers across her brow, she didn't wince or reel from the sharp pain of an open wound. In fact, she didn't feel any slice in her skin at all. Confused, she rose from her knees, slightly unbalanced, and staggered her way to the bathroom. Glimpsing her reflection in the mirror, she was shocked to see that, other than a minor bruise on her forehead and a couple of spots of crimson speckled across her cheek, there was no other blood. She appeared to be uninjured. But the book.., the blood.

She wasn't imagining it; the blood on her face and hands was evidence of that. But if not from her head, then where..? She froze for a minute as the color rushed from her face, and her hands began to tremble. Where, indeed?

That was the story Rebecca told me when she and I used to talk. Of course, that was many years ago, before I retired. I don't think she ever came to realize I had already known the story before we had ever met. How could I not have? After what she had done, Rebecca Fenton had been the lead story on every major newscast in the city. It disgusted me at the time. I was one of the men cheering when I heard how the police forcefully dragged her out of her apartment in handcuffs. It was her neighbor in the next apartment over that had alerted the authorities. When he was interviewed, he said that, although it had been very aggravating, listening to her newborn baby crying at all hours of the night, he was sympathetic and knew it would eventually stop. He just never imagined it would stop because of such a horrible incident. He later stated that Rebecca had always seemed so sweet, but when he heard the awful sounds coming from her apartment that morning, he knew something was very wrong. It wasn't until the trial that we all learned of her mental illness. It's a shame she didn't get the proper treatment until it was too late. That was how *we* first met.

She went away for many years, housed in the same institution where I had worked as an orderly, where she could be watched and cared for, especially after she learned what she had done to her own baby. Admittedly, even having been in my position, I was at first sickened by the events. But over the years, as I had gotten to know her, I had learned to understand. It hadn't been Rebecca's fault.

Many would later debate how the system had failed her, but that wasn't true. She had an illness that haunted her more than even she knew about, and because of it, another innocent was lost. No, two innocents were lost.

The screams that later came to her while under my care were those of self-torture and regret as she relived the events of that morning in the bitter nightmares that haunted her sleep. She still heard the screams of her baby crying, biting into her soul. She couldn't let them go; they were all she had left of her child.

Years later, after I retired, that woman still managed to find her way into my thoughts, now and again. I often wondered how she was doing, if the screams had finally subsided. Had she learned to forgive herself for what she had done? And now, perusing the morning paper, I read that Rebecca passed away peacefully in her hospital bed. She was fifty-seven years old. She had no family, so there won't be a service, and I doubt there will be anyone at her burial. Well, maybe I'll make an appearance.

It's sad to think that, to most folks, she'll only be remembered for one thing: the tragic event that captivated this small city for a time. As for me, I try to look for the positives in all the negatives this world throws at us. Rebecca has finally shed her mortal shell and left this world for a better place; one where she will no longer have to worry about listening to the horrifying sound of screams in the dark.

12

Night of the Forge

The fog was as dense as he'd seen it, the way it clung to the dirt road he'd been traveling on for what seemed like hours. Really, it had only been thirty-five minutes, but with the only scenery of note being the towering rows of cornstalks on either side of the road and the reflection of his headlights against the thick, pallid wall of haze in front of him, time seemed to march along at a crawl.

He should have known better than to listen to the voice from his GPS when it told him to turn down the desolate-looking stretch of road he'd now been on since straying from the paved city street. Night hadn't fallen at the time, and the fog hadn't yet rolled in, so the audible request didn't seem too intimidating. He wouldn't have thought the unpaved trail would have gone on as long as it had, yet here he was still wrestling with the steering wheel as it wobbled in his hands from every rock, bump, and rut in the road he was unable to avoid.

He blamed Stacy, his co-worker he'd met up with at the conference. It was her idea, suggesting he drive on the business trip instead of fly. *"Take in the sights,"* she said. *"It'll do you some good."* Even when leaving the conference center to head back, she stopped him to reiterate her earlier statements.

"John, I'm glad you listened to me and decided to drive. You've been working way too hard lately. Now, don't you dare rush back; take the extra day. Live a little. Turn off the highway setting on your GPS and let the road take you where it takes you."

What a great suggestion that was, he thought, as he peered through his windshield, struggling to see the road even five feet in front of his vehicle since the sudden arrival of the enveloping fog. It hadn't been that bad when it was still light out, but since the sun had gone down, the darkness only added to the eerie feeling of the long, lonely drive.

Although the lack of visibility was a hindrance, John sped up a bit, hoping to get back more quickly to somewhere resembling civilization. He had only seen one other vehicle since first turning onto this long stretch, and that one appeared to have been a car filled with raucous teens who were probably out joyriding or perhaps, partaking in other questionable activities, such as underage drinking within the secluded blanket of the cornfield. He couldn't cast too harsh a judgment upon the locals. After all, he had done the same a few times, himself, when he was younger, partying with friends in a clearing, away from prying eyes and under cover of the tall stalks. It certainly brought back some memories.

Whether it was from the distraction of his wandering thoughts or the near-sightless conditions he'd been driving in, John didn't notice the figure standing in the road until he was already upon the shadowy form. He slammed on his brakes and swerved to the right to avoid hitting the person, but because of the speed he was traveling, he lost control of the wheel, clipping the person with his driver's side mirror as he veered off an embankment into a ditch on the side of the road.

After overcoming the initial shock from the crash and realizing he was unharmed, John became stricken with panic, thinking he may have just severely injured someone else. Releasing his seatbelt, he stepped from his car to check on the person he hoped wouldn't need medical attention. The fog had become so thick that as he made his way back onto the road, he couldn't see where the person was or if they had fallen to the ground. Slowly shuffling forward, waving his hands in front of him as if stumbling around in a dark room searching for the light switch, he called out:

"Hello? Are you all right?"

He received no reply, which only heightened his nerves.

"Are you injured?" John shouted. "Can you make some noise? I can't see you."

Much like before, there was no verbal response, but the subtle sound of a shoe scraping across the gravelly road behind him caught his attention. He quickly turned, wondering how he had managed to stumble past the person without seeing them. Through the intense haze, John could see a person standing several feet from him, but only that of their silhouette, which was blurry, at best, and which appeared somewhat distorted.

"There you are," John said, relieved the person was still standing. "I'm really sorry about that," he continued as he approached the silent figure. "Are you hurt at all?"

As he got within clear sight of the person he had struck, he realized why the person's silhouette appeared to be indistinct. He had thought the heavy fog had been playing tricks on his eyes, but as the stranger came into view, the truth was more horrifying.

Standing in the road between John and his car was a horribly disfigured man (at least he believed it to be a man since the person wore only a pair of shorts and no shirt), whose face and upper body had severe scarring as if from having been burned in a fire. As startling as that initial vision was, it wasn't the most shocking feature of the man's appearance. The man had only two appendages: a right leg and a left arm. John was, at first, taken aback at the astonishing sight, his thoughts immediately jumping to an irrational conclusion that the minor impact from his mirror had somehow severed the man's limbs. He opened his mouth to speak, but before any words could come, the disfigured man lunged forward and slammed his palm into John's chest with incredible force, sending him tripping over his feet and crashing to the ground.

Shaken from the hard landing, John angrily let slip three words, "What the fuck?" just before the figure bent down and grabbed ahold of his ankle. Gripping tightly and giving a fierce tug, the man with only one arm nearly dislocated John's leg with just one pull. Letting out a scream, John instinctively kicked with his other leg, striking the man's wrist and causing him to release his hold on him.

"What's wrong with you?" John shouted as he slid backward on his butt a few feet to distance himself from the one-legged man. The stranger stared intently at John who was slowly making his way to his feet.

"What the hell, man?" John raged. "It was an accident. I didn't see you in this shit."

The man stood silent, unmoving.

"What were you doing in the middle of the road, anyway?" he continued, trying to shift the blame, reasoning it wasn't his fault alone that the accident occurred. "Especially in these conditions," he added.

Without a word, the disfigured man pointed at John's left leg, the leg he had just yanked a moment before, and then hopped forward, reaching for John with his one scarred arm.

Feeling threatened, John reeled from the stranger's outstretched arm and staggered back. An intense pain shot through his left hip and leg.

"Hey, what the hell is wrong with you?" John questioned angrily, grabbing his left thigh to ease the throbbing that had begun.

Once again, the one-legged man pointed at John's leg and hopped menacingly forward. Avoiding the man's second attempt at grabbing him, John quickly side-stepped and made a beeline toward his car, doing all he could to ignore the pain in his leg. He hobbled to the side of the road while shouting at the horrid-looking man.

"You're frickin' crazy, dude. I was trying to help."

So intent on getting back to his car where he had left his phone, John hadn't realized the disfigured man had begun to hop after him. Just as he got to his open door and reached for the phone, he felt the fingers dig into the center of his back. Having no time to react except for wincing from the pain, he was suddenly yanked backward from the car door and thrown against the small embankment his car had driven off.

Dropping to one knee, John looked up at his horribly-scarred assailant, the silent figure looming over him threateningly while maintaining a deliberate stare on John's left leg. Confused and fearing for his life, John's "fight or flight" instinct kicked in, and he pounced forward, shoving the strange man against the side of his car, dropping him to his one knee. Surprised by his own actions (he hadn't known himself to be of the "fight" mentality), he paused for a moment, questioning what he had just done to this seemingly disabled person. It was a fleeting thought as he realized this was no time for moral judgment against himself;

the disfigured man, disabled or not, had come at him twice now, knocking him to the ground. He glanced at the open driver's side door, and the thought instantly came to him.

Reaching for the dash to the left of the steering wheel, John pressed a button and listened for the familiar sound of the trunk popping open. He couldn't believe it had come to this or even that a situation would ever arise that would require such an action he had now considered. Still, if there was one thing he had learned from his Boy Scout days, it was to "be prepared." Limping past the fallen man who, at that moment, was utilizing the back door's handle to pull himself to his feet, John reached into the vehicle's trunk and pulled out a wooden bat he had kept within for just such emergency purposes. He had no intention of using it, figuring the sight of it would be enough of a deterrent for an unarmed (or, in this case, *one*-armed) attacker.

As the severely-scarred man reached his feet and turned in John's direction, John raised the bat overhead with an accompanying verbal threat.

"All right, asshole; you better get the fuck out of here. I mean it; don't make me do something we'll both regret."

They were strong words meant to scare the one-legged individual, but instead, the grotesque figure bounded toward John with malicious intent. Shocked by the man's audacity, John swung the bat at his attacker's hideously disfigured face, meaning only to hit him light enough to let him know how serious he was.

With incredible reflexes, the one-armed man caught the barrel of the bat in his hand and yanked it from John's grasp, practically displacing John's shoulder along with it.

With the stranger now in control of the only weapon John had at his disposal, the "fight" response John once had suddenly diminished, and his "flight" response quickly emerged. He backed away from the stranger, glancing over his shoulder at the raised embankment. It wasn't going to be an easy effort making it up the mound going backward, but he didn't dare take his eyes off the threatening man. It was then that the thought occurred to him. How the hell did the one-legged freak even get down there without so much as losing his balance and falling into the ditch? It was a question that would have to go unanswered as the disfigured man, now with the bat in his hand, hopped forward, his intentions all too clear.

Just then, from above where they were standing, a vehicle suddenly passed by, startling John. He hadn't heard it approaching as his attention was focused elsewhere, and with the fog as thick as it was, he understood why the driver probably hadn't noticed them off the road. It did, however, cause the scarred man to turn his attention away as he watched the car's tail lights quickly fade into the distance. Sensing the distraction might be his best, if not his only, opportunity for escape, John turned and hurriedly crawled up the mound of earth to the more solid dirt road. As he began limping in the direction of the rapidly-vanishing car, he watched in shock as the strange man effortlessly bounded up the wall of dirt as if he had practiced it a thousand times before. John's adrenaline kicked in, and he quickened his pace, ignoring the throbbing in his hip and leg.

Suppressing the pain, John hobbled along the dirt road for what seemed like a mile, believing he had finally discouraged the crazy person from following. The eerie fog had begun to clear just as he approached a small wooden, one-lane covered bridge spanning a small ravine carved out of the land by a slow-running stream. Situated on the far side of the landmark, John spied a teenager, sitting idle on his bicycle, tossing stones into the stream below. A surge of excitement shot through him as it had been the first sign of civilization since first turning onto the dirt road or encountering the strange man who had violently assaulted him. Surely, he thought, the boy lived close by and therefore must be close enough to others who could help him with removing his car from the gulch.

John shambled across the bridge in a struggled sprint, catching the boy's attention about halfway across. John raised his hand with a friendly wave and called to the boy.

"Hey there. Hello."

The boy said nothing as he continued to stare, tossing another stone into the rushing water as John neared. Even as John arrived at the other side, the boy remained silent, peering over John's shoulder at the dwindling wall of fog.

"Hi," John greeted the boy a second time while trying to catch his breath, "I need a little help. My car is off the road back there in a ditch," he threw his thumb over his shoulder from the direction he came, "and I'll probably need a tow. Do you know of someone who might be able to help me out?"

The boy leaned to one side and glanced over John's shoulder to where John's thumb was directing his attention, and when he did, the boy's expression suddenly changed. John turned to see what had grabbed the boy's interest even though he knew immediately what it must be.

Appearing from the gray cloud of haze, the persistent disfigured man hopped forward, still carrying the bat he had relieved from John.

"Oh shit!" John blurted, watching from a distance as the figure strode onward with surprisingly more ease than would seem possible. The strange man had obviously been without a leg for some time based on how smoothly he carried himself without the aid of crutches.

"That's the guy that caused my crash," John said. "Then he attacked me. We should get out of here."

John shuffled past the boy while grabbing the boy's sleeve, hoping to coax him into following, but the boy stayed glued, watching the approaching man in dumbfounded curiosity. John tugged at the teenager's arm again.

"Let's go, kid; that guy's crazy. He's been following me."

The boy yanked his arm back, disinterested in leaving his post.

"Come on," John yelled, taking a step backward, "he's almost here."

"So go on, mister," the boy replied, shrugging off John's warnings. "I ain't scared. Besides, you said he was following *you*, not me."

John shook his head in frustration at the youth's ignorance as the one-armed, one-legged man continued across the bridge. John took a few more steps away from the boy as he pleaded with him to ride off, but the boy just shook his head in defiance. It was clear the boy wasn't going to let the scarred man scare him away, and John couldn't force the boy, who he figured to be about fifteen, to do something he didn't want to do. So, as John turned and began to create distance between himself and the approaching stranger, he hoped the boy was right about it being *him* the man was after, but a few moments later, he found that not to be the case.

The disfigured man was not after John specifically but something else instead. Having managed to distance himself from the covered bridge, John was unable to help the teenager when the bat-wielding lunatic struck the boy in the head, knocking him off his bike. The boy was unconscious before he even hit the ground.

John paused his retreat, even taking a few steps toward the disgusting scene, thinking he needed to intervene, but that was before he witnessed what happened next.

The disfigured man stepped on the boy's right pant leg, reached down and grabbed the youth's left leg, then yanked aggressively, severing it from his body. John keeled over from the sight and sound of the flesh tearing away, covering his mouth with his hand to prevent himself from throwing up, all the while watching in horror as the disturbing scene continued unexpectedly.

The sickening man brought the teenager's leg to his own hip, where only the stump of a previous appendage resided. Sinewy flesh and muscle began to swirl and mingle with the amputated leg, sewing itself together in a woven mesh of skin until it had become one with the man.

John couldn't believe his eyes. The disfigured man had somehow fused the boy's leg to himself, making it his own. He now had two legs, but one of them was a fake, a forgery, a vile replacement for the real one. John now knew what the man, or more probable, the *thing*, was after. He needed parts to rebuild himself, stealing limbs from others so that he could be made whole. He was a living forge. And as John watched the Forge reach for the boy's right arm, knowing what was about to take place, he knew he needed to act.

"Hey!" John screamed, waving his arms in the air to get the man's attention. "Over here, you freak!"

The Forge looked up, distracted by John's screams. John began to wiggle his right arm wildly in front of his body, rubbing it and pointing at it.

"Is this what you want?" he yelled. "You don't want that scrawny arm. Come and get this one."

The Forge stood motionless as if contemplating John's words.

"Well, come on then," John goaded, shaking his arm fervently.

The Forge took a step forward, his first on his new leg, forgetting about the boy and determined to gain a new limb more his size.

"That's right, asshole," John continued. "Come and get it."

John began to slowly back away, making sure to keep the grotesque being's attention on *him*. He couldn't let more harm befall the boy. As it were, he had no idea if the boy were even still alive, but if he were, he would require medical attention fast.

"Let's go, you ugly son-of-a-bitch. Come and get *my* arm."

The Forge stumbled forward awkwardly, unfamiliar with the use of his new leg. It was several inches shorter than his other, making it difficult for him to catch a normal stride. After many more lumbering steps, in which his advancement was at a much slower pace than before, the Forge paused and stared down at his new appendage as if confused by its lack of mobility. Relying on this new, shorter leg was not working out as expected. He reached down and grabbed the thigh of the new limb, digging his fingers through the pants fabric and into the meaty part of the muscle, and jerked on it with immense force. It didn't tear completely through the flesh with the first pull, leaving strands of skin and ligaments clinging together like a spider's web, but with a second tug from the incredibly strong figure, the leg ripped clean from his existing stump.

John witnessed every gory detail as the Forge tossed the still-bloody leg aside and hopped forward, the bleeding stump mending itself before his very eyes. Watching the one-legged man gain speed with his awkward stride, John couldn't help but stare in amazement for a moment. Somehow, the Forge moved more swiftly with only one leg than having two that were disproportionate.

John didn't know what was going on or why the creature (he surmised it couldn't be human) was so intent on chasing him down, but he wasn't going to stick around to let the Forge take one of his limbs. He also knew the boy was in serious need of medical attention and could die if he didn't seek help. So, he turned and ran down the street, passing by a sign that read, "Welcome to Sterns Bellows, population: 158."

He now knew why the people of this town seemed so scarce. He was used to big cities with populations in the upper tens of thousands, where people would be rubbing shoulders with each other simply by strolling down the sidewalks. With only 158 people in this backwater town, he wondered if there was even a hospital or small medical facility to aid the boy, or would he need to be transported to the next town over? Either way, he needed to find someone fast, but as he glanced over his shoulder, he saw that the Forge was still hot on his heels, hopping after him with uncanny speed.

As John passed by a couple of houses, he slowed to look for signs of life. There were no lights on, and they looked more like salvage yards, the way scrap automobiles and metal parts littered their lawns. Something that did catch his eye at the edge of the second property, however, leaning against a rusty oil drum, was an old machete.

Fearing he had no other option than to defend himself from the crazed thing that continued after him, John quickly veered onto the property to grab the well-used tool. He didn't know what else to do, but he couldn't wait around defenseless until the Forge caught up with him.

Grabbing the splintered, wooden handle, John noticed the rounded curve at the tip of the blade had broken off, leaving a jagged edge. The machete had certainly seen better days. Patches of rust decorated both sides of the once-shiny metal. The blade was dull and had gouges along its length, creating more of a serrated edge. It wasn't ideal, but it could still cut through flesh.

Wielding the weapon tightly in his sweaty hand, John stepped back into the street to face the fast-approaching lunatic. Staring at the Forge as he hopped menacingly closer, John felt his heart rate increase. He glanced down at the machete by his side and wiggled his fingers to make sure he hadn't gone numb. The shirtless figure, still wielding the bat, looked even more intimidating than he should, having only one arm. Having seen what the grotesque thing was capable of, however, John couldn't afford to be sympathetic toward the disfigured being. He wouldn't let himself underestimate its ruthlessness.

Gritting his teeth, John reached down and clutched the weapon with both hands.

"Come on, fucker, let's see what you've got."

And as the Forge stepped within striking distance and raised the wooden bat overhead, John swung the machete at a downward angle with everything he had, aiming for the creature's neck. With surprising speed, the Forge twisted the bat sideways, intercepting the weapon as the dulled blade dug into the bat. Lodged in the wood, John tried to pull it free, but the Forge twisted the bat forcibly, wrenching the machete from John's grasp. The Forge then swung the bat, with the machete still imbedded, at John, who barely managed to jump back in time to avoid the impact. A look of fear came upon John's face as he realized he had just relinquished his only weapon to the creature who was trying to kill him. Instantly, he felt his only recourse was to run from the crazed thing once again. Without another thought, he turned and sprinted away from the scene as fast as his injured leg would carry him.

The Forge paused in his pursuit, standing motionless in the street, then raised his hand to look at what he was holding. He tilted his head to the side like a confused puppy while looking at the two weapons as if processing what to do. The answer came quickly as the Forge flipped the bat upward and snagged the machete out of the air, trading one handle for another. Using the machete as a lever, he slammed the handle of the bat against the ground freeing the bladed weapon from its hold.

By the time he redirected his attention to his would-be victim, John was no longer in view, having detoured through a few yards to the next street over. It mattered little to the machete-wielding Forge. He wouldn't stop until he was made whole again. Slowly, but with inexplicable smoothness, he began to hop forward, scanning for the elusive man who had twice evaded him.

In just a short while, he stopped in his tracks and tilted his head skyward, hearing the soft, distant sound of a voice carried on the shifting breeze. It was coming from ahead of him, not far away, from a small house on the left. With a singular purpose, the Forge focused on the voice and continued forward.

"...keep on turnin', Proud Mary keep on burnin'. Rolling. Rolling. Rolling on the river."

Lamont Graves enjoyed the warm, calm evenings when he could sit on his front porch after dinner and relax in his favorite rocking chair, humming the tunes of his younger years. Now in his late seventies, he enjoyed the little things in life. Cataracts had taken his sight years earlier, but he was thankful for what he had: a house, a loving wife, and the songs of a bygone generation.

"If you come down to the river, I bet you gonna find some people who live. And you don't have to worry if you got no money..."

His singing was interrupted by a creaking sound in the old floorboards of his porch.

"Is that you Mabel?" Lamont questioned. "Are you done with those dishes already, come to listen to this tired old man of yours as he reminisces about the good ol' days? I can still belt 'em out like..."

Lamont never had a chance to finish his sentence before the chipped blade of the machete sliced across his throat, leaving him choking on his own blood. As his body convulsed uncontrollably while he clutched at the gaping wound in his neck, the Forge swung the machete a second time, hacking into the flesh just below Lamont's right shoulder. The blind man fell from his chair and squirmed helplessly on the porch floor, gurgling sounds spilling from his mouth just as blood spilled from his neck. The Forge took one more slash at Lamont's arm, successfully severing the limb. Paying no attention to the dying man, the Forge bent down and picked up the bloody appendage, then shoved it against the vacant stump of his own shoulder where an arm once resided. As before, tendrils of skin came alive, sewing themselves to the severed arm's ragged flaps left behind from the jagged edge of the machete. In less than a minute, muscle and tissue had fused, cartilage had melded between joints, ligaments and veins had connected as one, and the Forge had a new arm.

The Forge took a moment to admire his new limb, forming a fist and then reopening it several times to ensure it was in working order. Pleased with the feel of his newly-acquired arm, he switched the machete to his more dominant right hand and gazed down at the left leg of the now-deceased Lamont Graves. The Forge gripped the machete ever tighter, ready to act on his undeniable urge when suddenly, a piercing scream erupted from the doorway, startling the creature.

Lamont's wife had heard a disturbance coming from the porch and had gone out to check on her husband, never imagining she would find a disfigured, machete-wielding lunatic standing over his bloody corpse. As Mabel's screams rang out at the sight of the horrifying scene, the Forge reeled in pain, grabbing his ears to deafen the high-pitched screeching. The sudden shock and disorienting noise caused him to stumble back down the stairs and retreat from the ear-splitting annoyance, leaving two more lives destroyed in his wake.

A street away, John could hear the terrible screams echoing through the darkness, disturbing the silence. He knew what they meant; he had witnessed it first-hand. Another victim had been claimed, while *he* fled like a coward. A feeling of guilt washed over him as he bent down in the street to catch his breath, pressing his palms into his knees to prevent himself from falling over. Though he had no idea what it was or where it came from, the Forge had been after *him*. *He* was the one who ran and led the creature to this small town. *He* was the one responsible for the Forge terrorizing the unsuspecting people of this community. And as his chest heaved and burned, and sweat dripped from the tip of his nose, John closed his eyes, calming himself, realizing the decision he was about to make went against every fiber of his being.

He opened his eyes and stared for a moment at the several droplets of liquid by his feet, then stood and took a deep breath, feeling the cool air as it brushed across his damp face. He knew what he had to do and turned in the direction of the blood-curdling screams that still filled the night air. As John hobbled down the street, his leg still aching, he wondered what the creature had taken this time on his quest to become whole. It didn't matter. He needed to end the horror tonight. Based on the sound of the screams, it was too late to save whoever the Forge had stolen from, but he had to do all he could to prevent any more innocent people from being harmed.

Cutting through another yard just as the residents were stepping from their doorway to investigate the loud shrills, John threw his hand up and yelled to them.

"Get inside and call the police. There's a crazed killer walking the streets."

Hearing that and not recognizing the stranger crossing their lawn, the people quickly retreated into their home, locking the door behind them. John continued on his path, a renewed determination guiding his every labored step. He still had no idea what he was going to do once he encountered the grotesque being, only that he needed it to refocus on *him*. Perhaps he could gather enough strength to lure it back out of town.

A few moments later, John found himself back on the street where the screams had originated. He looked to his left down the long, vacant street, where the sound of the screams had since been replaced with hysterical sobbing. He then glanced to his right and saw the Forge, hopping in the distance, his effortless movement still a wonder to witness. He noticed the creature now had two arms, which explained the dreadful screams. It also served as a painful reminder of why he couldn't allow the Forge to continue on this path of destruction.

With his hip and upper thigh still burning, John hobbled after the one-legged thing to almost a slight jog, slowly gaining on it. He couldn't believe he was now chasing after the thing he had been running from since crashing his car in that cornfield. He couldn't help but think how different this night would have been had he not swerved to avoid what he thought was an innocent pedestrian. If he had the chance to do it all over again, he wouldn't hesitate to run the creature down, killing it on that desolate stretch of road before it could harm any more innocent lives. He couldn't change the past, but he was now willing to do all he could to ensure other peoples' futures.

As he closed the distance between himself and the deranged killer, getting within fifty feet of the machete-wielding lunatic and still unsure how to stop him, the Forge suddenly halted in the street, having heard John's approach. Seeing that, John froze for a moment before slowly continuing, his pursuit becoming more of a cautious shuffle. The Forge turned his head to the left, just enough to peripherally catch a glimpse of movement over his shoulder. The eerie sight of the Forge's disfigured features gave John pause as he felt his heart slam against his rib cage.

"That's right, asshole," John yelled, trying to sound braver than he was, "I'm coming after *you* now. How does it feel?"

The Forge twisted around to face John, pivoting on his one leg with incredible balance, a blank stare on his face, and the machete hanging by his right side. John took a deep breath and took a step forward, showing the creature he wasn't going to back down or run. The Forge's eyes shifted downward toward John's legs as he raised his left arm and pointed, signaling his wicked intentions. John swallowed heavily but didn't turn to retreat (even though every fiber of his being urged him to). Instead, he took a second step toward the creature, almost daring the Forge to attack him. The one-legged thing didn't disappoint.

Swiftly hopping forward several paces, the Forge raised his weapon overhead, his intended target almost within striking range. John gritted his teeth and somehow found the courage to hobble toward the looming threat, intent on stopping the creature or die trying. And as the gap closed, the Forge gripped the machete tighter, readying for his strike. But before he could swing the lethal weapon down upon his next victim, John lunged forward with both arms raised, bringing the offense to his attacker.

Aiming to catch the Forge off guard, John grabbed the creature's right wrist before he could react, while his other hand latched onto the grotesque thing's neck. With hardly a flinch, the Forge reached forward with his free hand and dug his fingers into John's bicep, tearing through the skin with incredible strength. Reeling in pain, John released his hold from the creature's neck just as the Forge slammed his palm into his chest, knocking him to the ground. The disfigured man stood over him ominously, ready to strike, his attention still fixed on the lower appendage he sought. Then, from behind the crazed being, the high-pitched sound of a siren rang out as a police cruiser turned onto the street, causing the Forge to falter and shake. He turned and brought his hands to his ears to dampen the awful noise as the cruiser came to a stop several feet away.

"Oh, thank God," John shouted, squeezing his injured arm, "help me!"

The policeman turned his siren off and exited the vehicle with his gun raised, his attention focused on the immediate threat of the one-legged man holding the machete.

"Drop the weapon and get on your knees!" the officer ordered.

No longer straining from the overwhelming shrieks of the siren, the Forge stood silent and still, gazing at the newcomer. The officer took a step forward, ordering the release of the weapon a second time. The Forge looked down at the machete in his right hand as if pondering the officer's request, then opened his fingers and dropped it to the road.

Having noticed the Forge's previous adverse reaction to the shrill sound of the siren, John yelled to the officer, "Turn the siren back on; the noise bothers him," but instead, the officer continued forward, reaching for his cuffs and demanding the Forge drop to his knees. The Forge remained motionless, only tilting his head to the side as if confused by the officer's words. And as the officer got close enough to try and force him to the ground, the Forge snatched his wrist with astonishing speed and wrenched it to the side, breaking the bones in two and causing the officer to drop his gun as he screamed in pain. Then, with his other hand, the Forge grabbed a fistful of the officer's hair and yanked it forcibly backward, immediately snapping his neck. The officer's lifeless body crumpled to the ground at the foot of the one-legged thing, who showed no remorse.

The annoying disturbance easily dispatched, the Forge turned to resume his assault on John, but as he did, the rusty blade of the machete dug deep into his thigh, causing him to stumble back and grunt in pain. The unfortunate distraction of the officer's death had allowed John to seize the relinquished weapon, and now that he had it, he wasn't about to lose it a second time. Hacking at the injured creature's leg once again, the Forge buckled and fell to the ground.

Once John had seen the killer go down, an uncontrollable rage overtook him. He reflected on the evening and everything that had happened. He thought of those who had been lost because of the horribly-disfigured man, and his blood boiled. And as his anger erupted in savage ferocity, again and again, the blade crashed down into the fallen man, tearing into flesh and hacking through cartilage and bone until all of the creature's limbs had been severed and torn asunder.

And as the rush of adrenalin began to fade from John's body, and he looked around at the horrifying scene he had left behind, his bloody hands began to quiver. He felt woozy and sick to his stomach. Everything around him started spinning, and he felt the machete fall from his hand just before he collapsed and the world went black.

It was the beeping sound that first woke him. He opened his eyes and looked around, his blurry vision trying to adjust to the light.

"Oh, thank goodness you're awake," a woman's voice rang out. "We've all been worried about you."

John blinked a few times, staring at the woman standing over him until her appearance came into focus.

"Stacy? Is that you? Wh-where am I?"

"Don't worry," she responded, "you're safe. You're in the hospital."

Just then, John remembered what had happened.

"Oh my God," he shouted. "The boy. Did he make it?"

"What boy?" Stacy replied, looking confused.

"The boy by the bridge," he answered hysterically. "That thing attacked him. It attacked all of us."

"What are you talking about, John?" Stacy questioned, a concerned look on her face.

"The Forge! That's what I called it anyway. It came after me; it wanted my leg so he could become whole. It killed people for their limbs. It killed a police officer. But then I killed it so it couldn't hurt anyone else. Not anymore. I left it in pieces."

"Oh, John," Stacy mumbled, a tear rolling down her cheek. "You don't know what's happened, do you?"

"What are you talking about?" he asked in an annoyed tone. "Of course, I know what happened. I told you, that thing tried to take my leg. It took body parts from people. Why won't you believe me?"

"John," Stacy said quietly as she peeled the sheet from on top of him, exposing the horrible truth. "You were in an accident. Your car swerved off the road into a ditch by some cornfields. You're lucky they found you in time. You had to be airlifted to the hospital. The surgeon did all he could, but he couldn't save them. He had to amputate your right arm and your left leg. I'm so sorry, John."

And as John looked down in horror at his disfigured body, he realized he had become the terrible thing he thought he had destroyed.

13

Serial

It's the blood, the liquid crimson of the fallen as it drips down their neck and pools beside their shoulder. It never fails me, never lets me down. It understands me when nobody else does. It calls to me, beckoning for release. How can I ignore its sweet whispers? The urge, the hunger, it's always present, and I want to feast.

Another one fell victim to my blade last night, a petite blonde, shapely but made up like trash. She had it coming; she deserved what she got. Another will fall tonight, perhaps a brunette or a redhead. I grow weary of the same fair-haired beauties after a while. But they never grow tired of my knife.

I remember my first, though it was so long ago. Dear sweet Venessa, with the way her golden locks fell about her bare shoulders, making me feel something I wasn't supposed to feel, she set me on this path. Her alluring smile captivated me, as I'm sure it had many others. It's why I had to remove her lips. But only after I cut off her feet so she couldn't get away.

Venessa will always be special to me; she was my first. I remember her beautiful blue eyes, the feel of her smooth skin, and every curve on her perfect body. I remember the clothes she wore as I held her down, pressing my weight upon her. I promised her it wouldn't hurt; I wouldn't let it. But some promises are hard to keep.

At the time, I didn't know it would be such fun. I never thought there would be others. I now know Venessa's sacrifice served as mere practice for what was to come, the artistry of my life's work.

There were a few others in the early days, just after Venessa, that I barely recall, nameless, faceless women, their silhouettes unrecognizable. Their indistinguishable features sometimes still haunt my dreams. I swore I wouldn't let myself forget another of my targets. That's why the souvenirs I take are so important. They are the subtle reminders of who the fallen ones once were.

The fingers are the easiest to take, though I've taken toes and an occasional ear, now and again. I store them in a jar in my closet for safekeeping. I pull it out once in a while, sifting through the trinkets of my previous slayings, recalling every vivid detail of my handiwork. They have all played a part in making me who I am.

Ginger was a shy one when it came to meeting men. You wouldn't know it by looking at her, the way she showed off her long, slender legs in those skimpy, skin-tight shorts. She gained *my* attention, though I bet she wished she hadn't.

Marge was another demure lass, never saying much. After spurning my advancements, I made sure she never said anything again. Taking my blade to the corners of her mouth, I sliced so deep into her cheeks that no amount of stitches would have made her whole again. Not that it mattered, I plunged my knife into her chest right after.

I was sloppy back then, utilizing a serrated blade. The wrong tool for the job. It made such jagged cuts as it tore through the outer layer of skin, ripping the flesh in such an ugly way, even for my tastes. But I learned quickly, developing my talents further, and by my sixth kill, I had graduated to a straight blade.

Steph was the unfortunate subject of its first encounter with the flesh. The slice across her throat was so straight, so clean, the wound so pristine. After its first taste, it wanted more. So, more is what I gave it.

Becky had strayed from the other girls with which she usually gathered. It wasn't her fault she was different from the rest. She came from a different place and never fit in with them. It wasn't from lack of trying; things sometimes didn't work out. She eventually relocated, but not far enough away that I couldn't find her.

Becky was a tough one; I'll give her that, made of sterner stuff than the weak ladies that had fallen before her. Still, I ended her as I had the previous six, lying naked and lifeless, a piece of her anatomy stolen to become a part of my growing treasure.

With each kill, my proficiency improved, and my confidence grew. I viewed every victim as simply practicing for the next. One by one, they fell to the cold, hard steel, their lives forfeit to the sharpened edge of my trusty blade. They never put up much of a struggle; I had learned that smothering them first takes the fight right out of them. At first, it was with a towel, but later with just my hand so I could feel their nose and mouth as they labored to take a breath. It was invigorating. It was easy. But maybe a bit too easy.

The women I had chosen were fun, and they were teaching me the necessary skills for this most desirable trade I had found myself in, but they were hardly a challenge. I thought of venturing out, expanding my horizons. I would try my hand at the less-fairer sex.

I wasn't as adept at choosing a man, unsure of what it was for which I was looking. The women made it easy, wearing their sleazy outfits and flashing their seductive smiles. The few men I shadowed were not as appealing. I decided to wait and continue to watch for a time until my patience eventually paid off. As it turned out, I didn't have to choose a man; he chose me.

I saw him one day, shirtless and full of arrogance, flaunting his chest and abs to the ladies. He had no shame, obviously trying to win them over. He needed to learn a lesson in humility, and I was more than willing to teach it to him.

I made a habit of learning my victims' names, not only to feed my curiosity so I could recall their glorious demise at a later date; it was because I was ending their existence. I felt I owed them as much.

I had learned the man's name was Ken, even introducing myself to him one day. Don't get me wrong; I'm not a pervert, but I had been keeping my eye on him to make sure he stuck around long enough to feel the sharp sting of my blade.

I waited for the right time to strike, at night and under the veil of darkness. He never saw me coming, and he never stood a chance. My hand covered his face, a homemade concoction of chloroform wafting from my palm, silencing any opportunity he had to scream. Once I dragged him away from any potentially prying eyes, his schooling began.

I took my time with that one, carefully planning every incision, every slash across his muscular form. Sadly, in the end, he was weak like all the others and perished just as quickly. He was hardly worth my time. My trophy would have been his penis, but when I removed his pants, I was shocked to discover he was a eunuch, the first I had ever known. It was a shame; it would have been a nice addition to my collection. I settled for his thumb, instead.

He was the only man I ever killed. I was left disgusted by the entire experience. It was then that I knew women would always be my favorite prey. Taking their lives was more enjoyable for me.

Seventeen of them, to date. Eighteen after tonight. And I think I've decided who it's going to be: Melanie, the dark-haired vixen. She was new to the area and hadn't yet made many friends. That was always a good thing; there were fewer people to miss her or question her disappearance once she was gone.

Even though I had already taken so many lives, the thrill of taking another never wanes. Even now, from the very thought of it, I can feel my heart racing with anticipation and my palms getting sweaty. It's a wondrous feeling, but the real rush will come later this evening when I take the unsuspecting female. For now, however, I bide my time and wait for night to fall.

I've taken to teasing my victims a bit; I never used to do that. I like to look in their eyes and witness the fear come over them when they realize what's about to happen. I understand now why others who had taken up this line of work delighted in the torture. It feels so much more rewarding. I cut them, letting them feel the sensation, to know what it's like to be alive. I imagine the thoughts that must run through their heads, wondering if they've ever truly lived. They know what's coming: their inevitable end. But I'm not a cruel person; I spare them the agony of the real pain by smothering them before I plunge my knife into their abdomen, sinking it deep and letting it taste their insides. Like I said, so very rewarding.

Melanie should be waking up soon; it's been almost two hours since I grabbed her and dragged her away to my secluded place, the place I use for all my kills. I walk around her body, lying so peacefully on the floor. She has no idea what's about to happen, but she will, soon enough. I rub my index finger down her thigh, starting at the edge of her leather mini-skirt down to her ankle. Why did she have to be like the others, trying so hard to get people to notice her? Naughty, little girl. *I* noticed you. I tilt my head and lick my lips, admiring her sultry shape, with her black high-heels and her undersized, red tank top. She's going to be a fun one to torture.

I'm getting excited; I need her to wake up. Time is ticking away, and I'll need to sleep soon. I kneel beside her left shoulder and brush the dark hair from her face. She looks so calm and serene. I almost don't want to disturb her slumber, but I must; it's *my* time to play.

I tap her gently on the cheek with three of my fingers. Wake up, my darling. She doesn't move. I smack her again, harder this time, remaining silent while my thoughts are screaming, "WAKE THE FUCK UP!".

She stirs, and I let out a sigh of relief. She opens her eyes and sees me kneeling over her, but before she can scream or move, I press my left palm over her mouth, and with my right, I bring the knife in front of her face, letting the glimmer from the overhead light reflect off the curve of the blade into her eyes. While still holding the knife, I bring my index finger to my lips, signaling her to remain quiet. It won't be long now.

I place the sharp steel against the outside of her shoulder and give it a tiny yank, just breaking the skin. Her eyes widen, and she tries to scream, but I've become too good at this game to let that happen. I press down harder with my palm, letting the back of her head feel the hardwood floor as it pushes up against her, resisting my weight. I scowl at her as a warning while I lower my knife to her stomach just below her tank top. Sliding my knife between the cloth and her skin, I cut into the fabric, tearing it asunder as I draw the blade upward. Let's see what you have under there, shall we?

She begins to squirm more violently than I had anticipated. I realize I'll have to end her sooner than I had hoped. I place the knife on the floor beside me and reach for the towel by Melanie's head. I look at her in disgust. She looks at me as if questioning my motives. Don't look at me that way; you brought this on yourself. You've made me do this. I wrap the towel over her face and lean into it with all my weight. I'd use my hand, but the towel delivers faster results.

In moments, her struggling has ceased. She's unconscious and ready for her final nap. I wipe my eyelid just before a bead of sweat drips into my eye. I wanted more time with you, Melanie, but I'm afraid your time has come. I straddle her topless form, appreciating her accentuating features as I raise my knife to finish the job. Just then, my door bursts open, causing me to jump to my feet.

"Francis Matthew!" her voice boomed. "What do you think you're doing?"

"I told you, Mom," Emma cried. "I knew he was taking my dolls."

"Is that true, Francis?"

Before I had a chance to reply, Emma jumped in once again.

"He's been taking them and hurting them, even cutting parts off them. I found Cecely in the trash this morning. Her stomach had gashes, and she was missing two fingers."

My bratty little sister had a flair for the dramatic. I barely cut into the last one. But that didn't matter to my mom, who held out her palm when she saw what I was holding.

"Hand it over, mister."

"But Mom!" I cried.

"You heard me, Francis. There will be no more of this play. Those dolls cost money. How would you like it if someone ruined your things? Now, hand it over."

My head dropped in disappointment as I closed my Swiss Army Knife and placed it into her awaiting palm.

"Now, you apologize to your sister, young man."

I no sooner got the words "I'm sorry" out of my mouth than Emma stuck her tongue out at me and ran over to Melanie. Mom glanced over my shoulder.

"Is that our ketchup bottle on the floor?" she questioned? "You pick that up right now."

I walked over and grabbed the half-empty bottle, making sure I gave Emma a nasty look along the way. When I walked it back over, Mom grabbed my arm and forcibly yanked me.

"Let's go," she said. "You're going to put that in the fridge where it belongs, and then, you're going to wash up for bed. And tomorrow, there's going to be a whole list of chores for you to do to start making up for what you did to your little sister's dolls."

As she pulled me from the room, I looked back at Emma, stroking Melanie's thick, black hair. I felt a smirk come to my face. Oh, Sweet Melanie. You've escaped me this time, but I'll get you eventually. I'll get all of you. After all, your sacrifices will serve as mere practice for what will later become the artistry of my life's work. I'll perfect my trade.

14

Freezer Burn

For seventeen years, he'd worked there. The smell no longer bothered him; he had become desensitized to it after his first few weeks on the job, pushing the slabs of beef hanging from the tracks in the ceiling to make room for the incoming shipment. The work wasn't anything fancy; he wasn't going to get rich, but it was a living; one that paid his rent.

When Leonard applied for the job all those years ago, he never dreamed he'd still be there seventeen years later. He had never been one for long-term commitments. The "Help Wanted" sign above the door at the meat packing plant was only ever meant to be a few months worth of checks, enough to get him out of the city.

He remembered looking up at the red and yellow sign, a cartoonish image of a T-bone steak plastered above the words "The Butchery." It was one of the many meat packing plants just outside of Jersey City.

The Butchery packing plant was owned by a weasely Italian businessman who lived on the west coast. He had several plant locations across the U.S. but rarely visited any of them, choosing instead to let the managers of each plant run things as they saw fit while he cashed in on all of their hard work. As long as things ran smoothly, there was no need for him to get involved.

"The Butchery," Leonard thought while shaking his head, watching the early morning news on CNN. "Debauchery" would have been a more appropriate name after learning what they did with the meat back when he had first started.

The heavy slabs of beef used to be stacked against the back wall, resting right on the filthy concrete floor. They never got washed down before landing on the chopping table, where the employees would hack at them with machetes, cutting them up into smaller pieces for packaging. The employees rarely wore masks back then, so every cough and sneeze splattered liquid germs across the raw, bloody hides of the carcasses. Sweat would drip from the workers' foreheads and chins into the wheeled carts holding the cold slabs as they were loaded into the walk-in freezer. He guessed they all just figured that the bitter cold within would kill anything left behind. Nobody ever washed their hands after visiting the restroom, just picking up where they had left off handling the meat. He used to catch Charlie picking his nose all the time and, on more than one occasion, had witnessed him wiping his tainted fingers on the beef to remove the nasal remnants. None of that ever stopped Leonard, or any of the men, for that matter, from taking home their weekly allowance of free steaks. It was the only perk of the job.

Things had gotten much cleaner since then. Health Department regulations had become more strict. Guidelines and safe handling procedures had been put into practice to ensure sanitary conditions. Masks, gloves, hairnets, aprons, they had all become required protective wear if you wanted to keep your job. Some men moved on; most stayed. It was the free steaks.

Leonard had always been a diligent employee, eventually working his way up to Foreman, and then, when his boss Sal retired, he became Manager of the east coast plant.

Lately, Leonard had been feeling like he was getting burned out. The job wasn't what it used to be. The new foreman he'd hired, Mack, was a real piece of work, always complaining how it was unfair to hold the men accountable for every ounce of meat that accidentally hit the floor. He was a good worker, and for the most part, he kept the other men in line, but he didn't understand the pressures of the business. It wasn't like in the past when you could just pick up the piece of meat and place it back with the rest of the sliced-up herd. With the harsh restrictions and the hefty fines imposed on the food industry, anything hitting the floor had to be thrown out. You couldn't even thoroughly rinse it off, hoping to salvage the loss. And, although it was unfortunate, if you were the lug who had dropped the tasty morsel, it was immediately weighed before disposal, and the amount was subtracted from your weekly allowance of take-home food. Leonard had made it abundantly clear; that the business was no longer going to foot the bill for its careless workforce. It did, however, teach many of the workers to be more mindful, so there was much less waste of the delicious meat.

It wasn't only Mack's stubborn attitude, Leonard thought as he stood from his recliner in his darkened, dusty apartment. Some of the others had been getting on his nerves as well.

Harry, for instance, was constantly ranting about his personal life, questioning when he was finally going to find a female acquaintance so the others would stop harassing him about his sexual orientation. It was playful jibes, nothing so serious that warranted reprimanding or the need for sexual harassment training, but the man never stopped. It was like he enjoyed the attention.

Frank was another character who had issues. He had worked there since before Leonard was hired and had never liked him from the start. He rarely interacted with him, if he could help it, and only did when he was ordered to do so. Otherwise, the man wouldn't even look in his direction. Leonard never understood why; he hadn't done anything to Frank in all the years they had worked together. Once Leonard was promoted to Foreman, Frank's attitude soured even more, probably because *he* had expected to get the job. Then, when Leonard became the manager and overlooked Frank for the foreman position, hiring Mack instead, Frank shut down for a few days, choosing to work at a snail's pace. Some people were just like that, Leonard figured. It was why Frank was never seriously considered for the promotion, to begin with.

Marvin, or Marv as he preferred, was just a total asshole. He was offensive to everybody all the time. He didn't give a lick about his co-workers or their feelings. If you needed help with something, he wasn't the man to call for aid; he'd flat-out refuse, calling you a panty-waist or something of that sort as he walked away. Even though Leonard was now the boss, he always tried to stay clear of that one.

Then there was Clem. He was a weird one. He was a twenty-something who had just started six months earlier and, for some reason, thought it would be appropriate to start playing practical jokes on many of the old-timers. More than once, while hosing down the tables, he would "accidentally" spray someone in the back, blaming it on a muscle spasm in his arm. The boy was a bit twisted too. He once hid one hand in his sleeve, stained the white cuff with cow blood from the chopping table, then screamed to high heaven to get everyone's attention. The rest of the crew turned to see the kid holding a machete in one hand while his other looked like a bloody stump as if he'd just cut his hand off at the wrist. They were only harmless, little pranks, but they became annoying after a while.

Leonard shook his head in frustration as he opened his refrigerator door and pulled out an eight-ounce steak he had been marinating for the morning's breakfast. Steak and eggs had become a staple diet of his for many years now. He was hungry and wanted to eat, especially after the previous night he had had, but the sight of the steak made his stomach turn. He had been having too much of it lately, and it only served to remind him of work. Even so, the meat had never made him feel sick before. As he suspected, he was probably getting burned out. What's worse, he had hardly slept the night before, and when he *had* managed to drift off, he kept having vivid dreams of being at work and chopping up the bloody meat. It was the first time in all the years he'd worked there that he'd had such horrible visions.

Despite the unwelcome dreams and the negative thoughts about his coworkers, he had woken up in a good mood. He wasn't about to let them ruin his morning. He thrust the off-putting thoughts from his head and plopped the steak into a frying pan. As it began to sizzle, he imagined the ill feeling in his stomach would go away after the first bite. Steak always made him feel better, especially since it was free. It was the only perk of the job.

After breakfast, when Leonard's stomach had calmed, he headed out to open up the plant. He was an early starter, always arriving an hour or so before the others. He liked to begin each morning with a unique ritual without anyone else around for fear they would think he was crazy. He opened up the walk-in freezer door and stepped inside.

"Good morning, Bessy," Leonard said as he walked by the first side-of-beef hanging in the freezer. Over the past few years, he had taken to naming them. Females were Bessy, males Bernard. "Hello, Bessy two. Good to see you, Bernard. Hi there, Bessy three; you're looking good today. Bernard two, how's it hanging? Bessy four, my dear; always a sight for sore eyes. Bernard three, you're a ladykiller."

He stopped halfway across the floor, glaring at the remaining slabs hanging before him, and suddenly remembered why it was that he awoke in such a good mood. A smile came to his face as he continued his odd morning ritual.

"Howdy there, Bernard four. What's shaking, Bessy five? And how are you this morning, Harry? Hey there, Mack, you're not looking so good. What's going on, Frank? Clem, my man, never looked better. And Marv, you're still an asshole."

He reached the far wall and turned to look at the frozen slabs of dead meat hanging from the iron hooks in the ceiling. He had a full day's work ahead of him. There were five extra carcasses that morning that needed to be chopped up into smaller portions. Leonard's mouth began to water at the thought of the delicious meat he'd be taking home. It was the only perk of the job.

He'd hang the "Help Wanted" sign in the morning.

15

Clinical Trials

"Would you like to try again out of the same batch of samples, sir?"

"No, I think I've had enough out of that batch. Nothing seems to be working."

"Perhaps you just need to rest awhile, collect your thoughts?"

"I've rested long enough; I know I can do this."

"Shall I retrieve the next batch then, sir?"

"Yes, get me batch RVN-16. And a few more vials of Trepinome."

"Right away, sir."

"I'm so close; I can feel it. What am I missing? One of these samples has got to work. They can't all be bad."

"Here you are, sir."

"Place it down there, would you. Tell me, do you remember which batch it was that offered the most promising results?"

"I believe it was RVN-9, sir."

"Yes, yes. That's right; its chemical composition started breaking down only *after* it was exposed to the air. Tell me we have some of that batch still kicking around."

"We do, sir."

"Quickly then. Fill a syringe with that sample and bring it to me."

"Are you sure you want to do that? Mixing samples could throw off the data."

"Are you questioning me?"

"No, sir. It's just that.."

"I don't care about the data. The data means nothing if I can't produce a working sample. Now, go get me that syringe from the RVN-9 batch."

"As you wish, sir."

"What was it in that batch that remained stable for as long as it had? The Tricyllium? The Emoxin? It couldn't have been the Bifulopren; that caused RVN-7 to break down almost immediately."

"What was that, sir? Were you saying something?"

"No, I was just thinking out loud. Do you have the sample I asked for?"

"I do, sir."

"Give it here. I must study it."

"You know, sir, I've been thinking…perhaps this experiment of yours was never meant to be. I mean, look how much time and effort you've put into this already, and you still have nothing to show for it."

"That's precisely why I *must* keep going. I have nothing to show for it. Aha! Look at this in the microscope. Tell me what you see."

"Well, let's have a look. I'm sorry, sir, I don't see anything that would… wait, did it just..?"

"That's right."

"But, how..?"

"It must be the Trepinome. Each of the previous samples had already been mixed with the Trepinome before adding the Cillyseum. How long has this sample been in the cryo-chamber?"

"It's been on ice for almost three days now, sir. But I fail to see how that is relevant."

"Don't you see? This sample hasn't been mixed with the Trepinome yet. An untainted sample chilled to negative 4 degrees Fahrenheit for three days…"

"Of course. Without the thermal properties of the Trepinome reacting with this sample's natural resilience to cold, it had nothing to alter its bio-limiter. But will it break down once exposed to the air?"

"That, my friend, is what we're about to find out. The RVN-16 sample, please."

"You're not thinking about combining the two samples, are you?"

"I'm not just thinking about it; I'm *doing* it."

"But sir, the RVN-16 sample has already been mixed with the Trepinome. Didn't you just determine that was the issue?"

"The Trepinome is needed to form the cohesive bond within the sample. There's no getting around that. If my theory is correct, it only became an issue because of *when* the Trepinome was introduced into the subject sample. RVN-16's bio-limiter has already been compromised by the Trepinome. But, if I inject the virgin RVN-9 sample into the RVN-16, its frigid temperature should nullify the thermal properties of the Trepinome."

"You *do* have me curious, sir."

"Stand back. I have no idea how the RVN-16 will react when a foreign body of similar composition is introduced."

"Be careful, sir."

"I didn't get this far by being careful. There, I've done it. Now, we watch. Come on, come on. Don't break down on me."

"How long do we have to wait? How will we know if it worked?"

"If it hasn't turned green after two minutes, it's safe to assume it's stabilized."

"And if that should happen?"

"Then we add the Cillyseum as originally planned. The Cillyseum is the key. Without it, the entire experiment, everything I've worked to achieve, is pointless."

"I hope it works, sir."

"It has to. It must."

"Well, good news! We just passed the two-minute mark, and the sample is still clear."

"Yes! Yes! I knew it! Didn't I tell you? This is going to work. Hand me the Cillyseum. There's no time to waste."

"Yes, sir. Here you are."

"Now, we introduce the Cillyseum into the newly stable RVN-16 sample. There we go."

"I'm not seeing anything happening, sir."

"Give it a moment. Just a moment. Come on. You can do it. Just another moment. You can… There! Do you see it? Do you see what's happening?"

"Yes, I see it changing color."

"It's changing to a slightly pinkish hue, just as it's supposed to. It's working. This is incredible! I've done it! Look at it. It's truly beautiful, is it not?"

"It *is* magnificent, sir."

"Do you know what this means? I've unlocked the key. I've done something that's never been done before. Created something that's never been created before. It's perfect. Absolutely perfect."

"Um, sir. What's going on with the sample? Something seems to be happening to it."

"No. No, no, no. You can't do this to me. Not now. Not after I had finally done it."

"It appears to be morphing into something…strange, sir."

"Don't you think I can see that?"

"But what is it, sir?"

"I have no idea. This wasn't supposed to happen. It was working. I had it all worked out."

"I think it's stopped, sir. It's no longer changing."

"All the time I've spent concocting this notion that I can do something great. It's all been for nothing. You were right; I should have abandoned the idea long ago. Every batch, every sample, a failure. All of the trouble I've gone through, thinking this experiment would work. Instead, I'm left with this… this… whatever this disgusting thing is."

"I understand how disappointed you are, sir, but you mustn't let this get you down. There are other places you can go. This was just a minor setback. You'll eventually get it right."

"Perhaps, you are right, my friend. It wasn't for nothing. We learned what *not* to do. I can try again elsewhere. I'm right on the cusp; I can feel it."

"That's the spirit, sir."

"Thank you for all of your help and encouragement, dear friend. I appreciate everything you've done. However, I think I am ready to retire for the evening. Would you please be so kind as to clean up this awful mess? I can't stand to look at it."

"Of course, sir. But, what would you like me to do with this wretched thing you've created?"

"As you've done with all of my previous failures: dispose of it somewhere far away. I never want to think of it again. It repulses me."

"Yes, sir. I think I know just the place."

"Do you?"

"Oh yes, sir. I know of this dark, disgusting little place at the far reaches of the easterly galaxies, a putrid little vacant rock called Earth. I'll just toss this ugly thing there where it can waste its days away."

"Good. See that you do that then. I want nothing to do with my past mistakes."

"Oh, sir. I almost forgot. I'll need a name for this mistake so it can be logged into the books."

"Hmmm. Call the wretched thing human. Now get it out of my sight."

"As you wish, God."

16

Time's Up

Thomas couldn't help but stare at his watch in the final minutes, watching the secondhand tick away the last moments of his incredible adventure. He was amazed at everything he'd seen, all he'd encountered, yet saddened it was coming to an end, even in his unexpected present situation. And as the last twenty seconds ticked down, he reflected on the previous forty-eight hours of his life, where everything he thought he knew about his bleak reality came tumbling down, replaced with a renewed sense of hope with the press of a single button.

Ever the skeptic, Thomas leered with an unbelieving glare when his brother directed him to step inside the glass and metal enclosure that looked like a large canister one would find at the drive-thru of their local bank. The device wasn't hooked up to any pneumatic transport tube, however, instead, looking out of place among the normal items located in his brother's basement, such as the furnace, the washer and dryer, and the treadmill he was sure never got used.

When Thomas had volunteered to be his brother's first test subject should the device ever be completed, it was offered sarcastically, confident he'd never have to worry about such a thing. It was a ridiculous notion, the idea of creating a machine that could send a person back in time. It was the stuff of science fiction enthusiasts who couldn't grasp the concept that some things just weren't real. Yet, here he was, a year later, following through on his promise to his brother after he'd gotten the enthusiastic call, informing him the "Time Pulse Actuator" was ready. It was a horrible name, he thought, as he sat on the cold metal platen affixed to the inner wall of the device. He thought his brother could have done better, perhaps calling it a "Past Particle Accelerator," a "Time Stream Manipulator," or even a "Time Displacement Capsule." He would have suggested such alternative names, but he didn't want to play into his brother's misguided delusions that time travel was possible. It was almost embarrassing.

"Shouldn't there be some kind of seatbelt or harness that I can use to strap in?" Thomas asked jokingly as he stared at the elaborate console in front of him.

"The machine doesn't move, jackass," Dennis replied. "Your body will be bombarded by an ion pulse that will push your body back through time. Think of it as a matter disruptor."

"Yeah," Thomas said as he rolled his eyes flippantly, "that's what I was thinking was going to happen." He didn't understand any of the scientific jargon; that was for his brother, the quantum physicist, to worry about. He just knew his brother was going to overreact when the little experiment failed.

"So, tell me again how this is going to play out," Thomas said.

Walking over to the open door of the machine, Dennis tapped on the digital display mounted to the front panel. "You set the date you want to travel to on the monitor. Then, when you're ready, I'll hit the pulse actuator on my console station over there."

"Then what?" Thomas asked.

"Then, you'll no longer be here and now; you'll be in that other time."

"Sounds pretty simple," Thomas added. "That answers the *when*. But *where* will I be?"

"The ion pulse will push you back in time and place you as close to this same location as possible," Dennis answered.

"Isn't that dangerous?" Thomas asked. "I mean, couldn't I materialize inside of something?"

"This isn't teleportation, dimwit; it's time travel. An object's matter can't occupy the same space as another object's matter at the same time. It's perfectly safe."

"If you say so, little brother. So, how do I get back?"

"After you vanish, I will reset the date to the present and pull you back through. It will be instantaneous on my end, but for you, you will have visited the past for forty-eight hours."

"Two days? What am I supposed to do for two days?"

"That part is for you to figure out, brother. Just don't muck things up."

"Muck things up? What's that supposed to mean?"

"You know, don't try to change anything. You're not going back to try to become rich or anything, and you're not there to meet people. In fact, try not to interact with people at all if you can help it. Get yourself a place to stay, some food, and wander around. Enjoy the sights."

"Can I buy things?"

"Only things you plan on keeping back there; you can't bring anything back with you."

"Okay, got it," Thomas nodded. "Sounds like a boring trip."

Dennis shook his head. "Knock it off; this is an important moment for me."

"Okay, okay, I'm just teasing. I'm sure it'll be great." Thomas spoke the words but still had his doubts that anything was going to happen.

"And you've got cash?" Dennis inquired.

"Two hundred dollars. I hope it's enough. I wasn't expecting to be away for two days."

"You'll be fine," Dennis responded. "Money went a lot further in the past than it does today."

"That *is* true," Thomas agreed. "My grocery bill was through the roof last week. I remember when milk was a dollar sixty-nine a gallon. It's ridiculous."

"Depending on what year you decide to go back to visit, you may find the prices even better than that. So, when's it gonna be, then?"

"I don't know," Thomas replied, reaching for the dials on the display, "any random date should do. How about June 16th, 1958?"

"Sounds great," Dennis responded, walking back to his console station. "I can't wait to hear all about it. Are you ready?"

"As ready as I'll ever be."

Dennis took a deep breath, then pushed the blinking red pulse actuator button.

A smile came across Thomas' face, thinking how his little brother had done it. He had conquered time travel. And now, with only ten seconds left before his trip to the past came to an end, he couldn't wait to get back to tell his brother all about it. It had been amazing from the moment he'd first arrived, current circumstances excluded. The memories once again rushed back to him.

Suddenly appearing in a large empty plot between two houses, Thomas knew the machine had worked. He recognized both houses immediately as those belonging to his brother's neighbors. That's when it dawned on him that his brother's house didn't exist yet, having been built in 1960. Just as his brother had mentioned, he would arrive as close to the same location as possible; or in this instance, the *exact* location.

Thomas glanced at his watch to take note of the time. He had two days to kill and wanted to make sure he kept track so he wasn't around anyone when he was pulled back to the present. Seeing a person vanish in his own time would surprise someone for about two minutes until they dismissed it as being just another street performer's magic trick. But in 1958, seeing someone vanish would probably cause widespread panic, as the people of that era would believe the planet was being invaded by aliens or something to that effect.

He looked back up from his watch to take in his surroundings. It was calm, quiet. The houses on either side of him looked new and well-kept compared to the worn, dilapidated structures they'd later become. The normally-busy street he had become accustomed to was now devoid of traffic. He breathed in deeply; the very air itself seemed fresher than in his own time, having less air pollution from the fewer vehicles passing by. He shook his head and smiled.

"Dennis, you sonofabitch," he spoke under his breath, "you did it, little brother. You actually did it."

With the initial shock wearing off, Thomas knew he had to find a place to stay. He was only a mile outside the city, but without a vehicle, he'd have to start walking if he wanted to make it before sundown. Seeing that he was sixty-four years out of time, he was unfamiliar with the hours businesses kept or what businesses there would even be. In *his* time, there were three major hotel chains occupying a single block downtown, but he had no idea if they had been built yet in 1958. He, himself, wouldn't even be born for another two decades, which was a thought that dumbfounded him as he began his long stroll down the street in search of shelter.

Only ten minutes into his walk, Thomas was amazed at how far apart the houses were spaced from each other, unlike how they were in *his* time, where it felt so cramped just to walk out onto what little amount of lawn you had. He was also astonished at how infrequently a car would pass by, but when one did, the driver would give a polite wave in his direction. In the future, drivers were more often seen giving a different kind of hand gesture, usually accompanied by the obnoxious blaring of their horns or the yelling of obscenities. It was a comforting change.

Another eight minutes and several friendly waves later, Thomas reached the center of town. It wasn't the sprawling metropolis of the future, but it definitely showed signs it was heading in that direction, with the construction of several new businesses well underway, including the Tower Hotel, which he had hoped was already established. He had had a pleasant experience there a few years earlier with a lovely lady; it would have been nice to revisit and reminisce about that time in his life. Instead, he had to choose from the other two hotels that stood prominently in the distance, the roofs of each barely extending into the skyline yet still making other buildings around them seem insignificant in comparison. With the growth of the city on the rise and construction crews traveling in from surrounding cities, he hoped to find there were still rooms available.

It was getting late, and the sky was growing increasingly darker. The hustle and bustle of the city, though still present, was quickly winding down. As he walked down the sidewalk, nodding to each pedestrian who felt compelled to tip their hat to him as they strolled by, he couldn't help but think how things have changed so drastically in his present. In the time *he* was from, strangers would rather turn away from you than look in your direction, or if they did look, it was to give you a nasty glare. It was refreshing to see friendly people showing others kindness and respect.

Reaching his destination, Thomas stepped into the Vandermeer, the closer of the two hotels. He had never stayed there before but heard decent things about it. Of course, that was in his own time; he was sure the amenities would be more modest in this earlier time. Walking up to the front desk, he passed a young bellhop, no older than eighteen he surmised, rolling a cart of luggage. The young man was dressed head-to-toe in a red and white outfit with a sequin-lined red vest, complete with a round, cloth hat atop his head with a strap that buckled under his chin. Thomas smirked, thinking how people of his time would rebel against wearing such a uniform unless they were part of a Las Vegas show. He found it amusing as he approached the concierge, who wore a more reserved light-blue suit and tie.

"Welcome to the Vandermeer Hotel," greeted the man behind the counter. "How may I help you, sir?"

"Hi, I'm looking for a room," Thomas answered.

"Do you have a reservation with us this evening?" the man asked.

"No. No, I don't," he replied. "But any old room will do. I'll take anything."

"Well, let me see what we can do for you," the concierge stated, flipping through a notebook to Thomas' surprise, who had just then realized that computers were a thing of the distant future. "Ah, here we are. You're in luck, sir. We have only one room left. It'll be eight dollars a night. Shall I book it for you?"

"I'm sorry," Thomas replied, "did you say *eight* dollars?"

"Yes, sir. We *do* offer the finest amenities. I assure you; your stay with us will be quite comfortable."

"Oh, I bet it will," he responded, shaking his head in disbelief, understanding what his brother meant when he said 'money went a lot further.' "Yes, please, I'll take it."

"Very good, sir. And how many nights will you be staying with us?"

"Two nights, please."

"Ok, two nights it is," he said while scribbling in the notebook. "I'll just need your name and an initial deposit of eight dollars for this evening's stay."

Thomas reached into his pocket, pulled out a ten-dollar bill, and handed it to the concierge, who was also the hotel manager, as labeled on his nametag. "It's Thomas Marshall, and uh, Keep the change."

"Oh, I couldn't..."

"I insist," Thomas interrupted. "You've been a great help."

"Thank you, sir. Please allow our bellhop to get your bags for you." He snapped his fingers in the air, "Peter, come here, please."

"Oh, I don't have any bags," Thomas said. "It's just me. What you see is what you get."

The manager offered a confused look and then reached into a drawer to retrieve the room key for his guest.

"It's room 307. Third floor."

"Look at that," Thomas said, "an actual key. It never ceases to amaze me."

"Pardon me, sir?"

"Nothing. Just an ineffectual attempt at humor. Thank you for the key," he tapped it a couple of times on the counter, "I'll see my own way to the room." He then turned for the elevators just as the bellhop arrived after being summoned, causing Thomas to bump him with his shoulder.

"Oh, I'm sorry about that," Thomas apologized. "It's Peter, right?"

The young man nodded. "It's all right, sir; I'm fine. I've taken harder hits before. Shall I retrieve your bags from your vehicle?"

"Sorry, kid; no vehicle, no bags. I travel light. But I'll tell you what, you lead me to my room, and I'll give you a tip for your trouble. Fair?"

"You bet, sir," the young man said with a smile.

"Please, call me Thomas. I'm sure I don't deserve the title 'sir.'"

Without a word, the boy nodded his head sideways and started for the elevators. It was a short, quiet ride up to the third floor, where Thomas' room was the fifth door down the hall to the right. When they arrived, Thomas turned to the bellhop with a smirk on his face.

"Peter, if you don't mind me asking, what does your job pay?"

With a proud smile on his face, Peter answered, "I get seventy-nine cents an hour, sir, plus tips."

"Wow, that *is* something," Thomas replied, trying not to sound too sarcastic. "And what do guests usually tip?"

"A quarter most times; sometimes fifty cents."

"Well, I'll tell you what, Peter," Thomas said, smiling while reaching into his pocket. "Here's a five-dollar bill. And there will be another one just like it if you wake me up bright and early tomorrow morning. Let's say, 6:45. Fair enough?"

Peter nodded, a stunned look on his face as he studied the bill he received from the generous man.

"Thank you for the escort, Peter," Thomas continued. "Now, if you don't mind, I'm going to retire for the evening. I've got a big day ahead of me tomorrow."

Peter continued to stare at the money even as Thomas closed the door behind him.

The next morning, as Thomas focused on the brightly-lit numbers displaying 8:17 on the clock, he wondered why he hadn't gotten that early-morning knock on his door as expected. It didn't matter; it wouldn't ruin his day. He planned to roam around the city and take in the sights and sounds of the past. His first order of business, however, after stopping at a local diner for breakfast, would be to get himself a new outfit. He didn't feel comfortable wearing the same thing for two days. Even with the hotel offering laundry service, he had nothing to wear while they were being cleaned. And at 1958 prices, he figured he could get an entire outfit for less than twenty dollars.

Leaving the quaintness of his surprisingly comfortable room, Thomas took the elevator down to the lobby, where upon stepping out, noticed Peter stocking a linen closet with freshly washed towels. Casually strolling over to the preoccupied bellhop, Thomas cleared his throat, surprising the young man.

"Ahem. Hello, Peter," he began. "I was expecting that early knock on my door this morning. Was the tip I promised you not incentive enough?" he teased.

With eyes widened and face flush, Peter nervously replied while trying not to make eye contact, "Oh, uh, yeah. Sorry, sir." Then, he quickly closed the closet door and immediately began wheeling the linen cart away.

"Hey, Peter," Thomas called out. "Is everything all right?"

"Everything is fine, sir," he yelled over his shoulder as he continued down the corridor. "Have a good day."

Feeling it was an awkward moment but realizing whatever the boy was holding onto was none of his business, Thomas shrugged his shoulders and headed for the exit to start his day of exploration.

After breakfast, where he tipped the waitress handsomely for her service, he purchased a pair of finely striped, polished gray cotton slacks, a charcoal and red sweater shirt with a ribbed collar, two pairs of nylon-woven tan socks, and a three-pack of Mayo Spruce underwear from a men's department store located only two doors from the restaurant, neither of which still existed in his present. He walked out carrying a large bag by his side and an even larger smile on his face, spending only $13.87 for everything.

The rest of his day was spent wandering around the city, admiring the window displays of many of the establishments, occasionally going inside to peruse the aisles filled with new items that would be the admiration of many antique enthusiasts of his own time. When he wasn't looking for reasons to stop and browse through the local gift shops of the day, his eyes were fixed on the buildings themselves, appreciating the style and architecture of many of the smaller businesses along the strip. Thinking ahead to when he came from, he thought about how time had taken its toll on many of the structures that were still standing, and those that were newer or had been rebuilt over the years didn't have the same class as those he was seeing on his current sojourn.

The cars that packed the streets for everyday use looked like something one would expect to see at a classic Cruise Night auto meet. The people he passed by were friendly, offering courteous smiles or tips of their hats, with an occasional "How do you do" greeting. Everything was very much in contrast to the time he lived in, and if he had the opportunity, he could picture himself visiting this previous time again, but for a longer duration. But for now, the daylight was fading, and he still had another day in which to explore and be fascinated.

He decided to head back to the Vandermeer to change into his new clothes so he'd look more presentable before stepping out to grab a bite to eat. The entire walk to the hotel, he couldn't help but be in complete awe at his brother's incredible accomplishment. Something he thought would never be a possibility, at least not in his lifetime, was now not only possible but something in which he was able to partake. As unbelievable as it seemed, he was now a time traveler. The first, in fact.

He arrived back at the Vandermeer as the sun was making its lonely descent over the horizon. When he stepped through the large glass entrance door, he noticed Peter sitting in the lobby with uniformed members of the local constabulary, the young man's face showing signs of fear and concern. Thomas glanced to his left, where he caught the eye of the manager stationed behind the front desk, who immediately waved him over.

"What's going on over there?" Thomas asked, nodding over his shoulder at the scene in the lobby.

"It's nothing to concern yourself with, sir," the manager assured. "I'm sure it will all be worked out soon enough. Now then, I *would* like to settle the bill for this evening's stay, if you wouldn't mind."

"Oh, of course," Thomas agreed, reaching into his pocket. "I'm so sorry I didn't take care of this sooner. My mind has been a little out of time. That was eight dollars, correct?"

The manager glared at Thomas for a moment before speaking.

"That is correct, sir. It will be eight dollars."

"Right," Thomas nodded. "I'm hoping you can make change."

He unraveled a twenty-dollar bill from the bundle he held and handed it to the man behind the desk. Just as he did so, an officer appeared from around the corner and ordered him to drop the money and raise his hands while the other officers in the lobby jumped to their feet and surrounded him.

"What's going on?" Thomas asked in shock. "What's this about?"

The first officer grabbed Thomas' wrist and slung it behind his back while another officer cuffed him and grabbed him by the shoulder, leading him toward the sofa in the lobby.

"I don't understand what's going on," Thomas said as he cooperatively walked with the officers. "I think there's been some misunderstanding."

With no response, the officers sat Thomas down and stood over him like towering statues as the hotel manager slithered from behind the front desk and approached the group, an annoyed look on his face. Peter took his place beside his boss, staying just outside the perimeter of the huddled policeman, his features displaying as more distraught and torn.

"Will somebody tell me what this is about?" Thomas demanded, peering up at the officers staring down at him.

One of the officers reached into his breast pocket and pulled out a folded five-dollar bill, unfolded it, and presented it at arm's length to Thomas, who immediately surmised it to be the tip he had provided to Peter since they appeared to have been questioning the young man when he arrived.

"Is this the bill you gave to the bellhop?" the officer questioned.

"Is it against the law to offer a tip?" Thomas snidely replied.

"Answer the question, sir."

Leaning forward and focusing on the currency with squinted eyes, Thomas riposted "It appears to be the same, though honestly, it's hard to say. It could be anybody's."

"And how about these, sir?" the officer spoke more sternly as he held out his palm toward the upset manager, who responded by handing him two more bills. "Isn't this the ten-dollar bill you provided Mr. Carponte yesterday for your room?" He raised the first bill to allow Thomas to study it before pulling it back to raise the second. "And this is the twenty-dollar bill you just handed him moments ago."

"I don't understand," Thomas said. "Why is this a problem? What's going on here?"

The officer pulled the bill back and examined it. "You seem like an intelligent fella," he said. "But you know what I can't figure out? How you expected to fool anyone with this fake money?"

"Fake money?" Thomas questioned, confused at the accusation.

"What's the matter," the officer added smugly. "You didn't think people would notice? Most of the 'funny money' counterfeiters try to pass off at least resembles the bills they're trying to copy. This is some of the worst I've seen. The presidents' likenesses are all out of scale on these things. And look at this," he continued, smirking. "You couldn't even get the date right. This one here says 2017. This one's 2020. This other one is 2021. Not that I'm complaining; I wish all of you white-collar criminals made it this easy."

"Oh my God," Thomas stated. "Is that what this is about? I can explain; it's not what you think."

"Well now, that's what we're all here for, isn't it. Go ahead; we're listening."

Thomas looked around him at all their faces, but none stuck out more than Peter's, who seemed nervous and upset about the entire ordeal. He then took a deep breath and began.

"The reason the bills look different, why the dates are what they are, is because.." he hesitated. "I'm from the future."

An immediate snicker was heard from one of the officers while the others glared at Thomas with unbelieving eyes.

"I know how crazy it sounds. I'd have a hard time believing it too, but it's true. Please, just let me explain."

"Oh, please do," the officer said, smiling. "We'd love to hear all about it."

"I'm from the year 2022. In my time, the date is August 5th. That's when I left my present and appeared in yours."

"Will you get a load of this guy," one of the officers spoke out.

"No, you don't understand," Thomas continued. "I'm not making this up."

He continued to explain his unusual situation and how he ended up in the past. He spoke of his brother's amazing machine in the basement of his house and how it worked. He told them all that he was only in the past for forty-eight hours, and then would be transported back to his own time, where his brother will have pulled him back only moments after he left. He kept to the facts of his current situation, being careful not to offer any other details about the future, even when one of the officers jokingly asked him who the next five presidents would be. When he was through, he was under the impression that 1950s law enforcement was lenient enough that they'd let him go after confiscating his cash. Unfortunately, that was not the case.

"It was a nice story, chum. You've got quite the imagination. It's too bad passing counterfeit bills is a felony no matter what time you're from. You're coming down to the station with us."

"I'm being arrested?" Thomas questioned excitedly.

"Indeed you are, sir," the officer responded while grabbing Thomas' arm. "Please stand."

"Don't you have to read me my Miranda rights?" Thomas protested.

The officer paused for a second, looking confused as he glanced at his fellow officers, who shrugged their shoulders in silent response.

"Enough of your nonsense," he said, pulling Thomas forward. "You'll be spending time in the clink until a judge can see you. When that happens, take my advice; you might want to refrain from any of that crazy futuristic talk."

Thomas was marched past the hotel manager, who leered at him unforgivingly, while the young bellhop's sorrowful face told a different story. It was one Thomas understood, so he smiled and nodded at the young man to unburden him of his guilt.

As the night turned into day, sleeping in the tiny cell wasn't as bad as Thomas thought it would be, most likely because he knew he'd be leaving soon enough. Later that evening, he'd vanish from 1958 and be back in his brother's basement on August 5th, 2022. And with that thought, he smiled.

Thomas keenly stared at his watch as the final seconds ticked down, relieved that his shoes and watch weren't confiscated when he was booked and thrown in the cell. It certainly was a different time than his own, when they would have taken all his possessions and stored them away for safekeeping. He wished he'd had the opportunity to see more of the city, but with time travel no longer a thing of make-believe and fantasy, he could come back whenever he wanted. But for this being his first trip, he'd have quite the story to tell his brother in 3, 2, 1…

Nothing.

He hadn't vanished. He was still stuck in a jail cell in 1958. It was his own fault. He had been warned. *"Try not to interact with people at all if you can help it,"* his brother advised. Instead, he not only interacted with people, he told them much more than he should have.

On June 13, 1966, the U.S. Supreme Court handed down its decision in Miranda v. Arizona, establishing that all criminals be advised of their rights before interrogation. It gained national coverage.

When Peter Sidrey heard the news, it immediately brought his thoughts tumbling back to that day in 1958, when a stranger in the hotel he worked at, busted for counterfeiting and spouting about how he was from the future, asked to be read his Miranda rights. He had forgotten about it until the Miranda decision was the top story on every network. At that moment, he knew it was true. He recalled the story the man had spewed, about his brother inventing a time machine in his basement, allowing the man to travel back to 1958. It's why he had the strange money. Nobody believed the man back then, but Peter suddenly believed him in 1966.

In 2004, lying in the hospital, accompanied by his son and withering away from Pancreatic cancer, Peter unburdened himself by telling the story he'd held onto for so long about the time-traveling man. He explained everything to his son, including how time travel would become a reality on August 5th, 2022, and that his son would soon be able to go back and visit with him one day after he was gone. Twenty-seven minutes later, Peter succumbed to the cancer that had been eating away at him.

On August 5th, 2022, Dennis had just pressed the pulse actuator button on his time console when his doorbell chimed. Hurrying upstairs, he opened the front door to be greeted by an older man, perhaps in his mid-fifties, holding a crowbar in one hand and a small paper bag in the other. The man was looking sullen as he spoke.

"Is your name Dennis?" he asked. "You have a brother Thomas?"

"Yes, on both accounts," Dennis replied. "Do I know you?"

The man remained silent as he leaned the crowbar against his leg and unfolded the crumpled top seam of the paper bag. He reached in and pulled out a small handgun. Before Dennis had a chance to react, the sound of the gun firing ricocheted off the neighboring houses, and Dennis dropped to the floor. The man calmly stepped over Dennis' body and proceeded down to the basement, where the machine his father had told him about years earlier was humming with power. He had a strong belief that time was something that should never be toyed with. Someone would eventually change something in the past that would spell disaster for the future. He couldn't allow that to happen.

He knew the police would be there soon, so he worked quickly to dismantle and smash as much of the machine as possible with the crowbar until it could no longer be recognized as anything but a pile of scrap metal.

In 1958, Thomas sat up in the uncomfortable bed in his cell, his elbows pressed against his knees, and his face pressed into his palms. A day before, he had wished he could stay longer in the past, pleasantly enjoying the sights and sounds of an era that should never have been his to enjoy. And now, it would seem, he would be getting his wish. He would be spending many more years in the past; only, he'd be doing it from behind bars.

Other books by Jeff VanOudenhove

Dark Place
Book 1 in the Dark Series

Dark Lane
Book 2 in the Dark Series

Dark Queen
Book 3 in the Dark Series

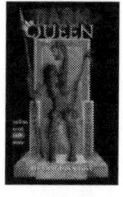

Dark Child
Book 4 in the Dark Series

The Final Dark
Book 5 in the Dark Series

SCREAMS
in the Dark
and Other Twisted Tales

Made in the USA
Middletown, DE
16 August 2022